RIDING SHOTGUN

DIRTY RYDERS MC SERIES BOOK 2

K.L. RAMSEY

Riding Shotgun (Dirty Riders MC Series Book 2)

Copyright © 2024 by K.L. Ramsey

Cover Design: Coffin Print Designs

Formatting: Mr. K.L.

Imprint:Independently published

First Print Edition: January 2024

All rights reserved.

No part of this book may be reproduced, scanned, or distributed in any printed or electronic form without permission. Please do not participate in or encourage piracy of copyrighted materials in violation of the author's rights. Thank you for respecting the hard work of this author.

This is a work of fiction. Names, characters, places, and incidents either are the product of the author's imagination or are used fictitiously, and any resemblance to locales, events, business establishments, or actual persons—living or dead—is entirely coincidental.

MELODY

Melody Newton didn't really know her self-worth. She was never taught to stand up for herself and she had the bruises to prove it. But now, she was going to get a crash course in what it meant to stand her ground and give a damn about herself. Now, she was going to finally tell her good-for-nothing husband to hit the road. She had caught him sneaking around on her again, and this time, she had no forgiveness left to give him.

Adam walked into the kitchen and kissed her cheek, just as he always did before dinner. That was when she'd make a fuss about asking him how his day was and tell him about what she and their two-year-old daughter, June, did together while he was supposedly at work. But that wasn't going to happen tonight because she knew where he had been all day. Adam had spent all afternoon at the sleazy motel on the outskirts of town with some whore he probably had picked up a disease from. Melody knew this bit of information because her loving husband had used his credit card to pay for both as if he just didn't give a fuck about her finding out what he was doing—or in this case, who.

"How was your day?" he asked.

"My day?" she questioned. "Well, my day was very exciting. You see, I took June to the grocery store to pick up some groceries," she started.

"Yeah, I was going to ask what was happening with dinner. You haven't even started it yet? And where is our daughter?" June was usually sitting in her highchair, anxiously waiting for dinner, but Melody had gotten her sister, Tilly, to babysit June for the evening, so that she could face down her soon-to-be ex-husband. That's how Melody was getting through any of this right now. She just kept thinking that Adam would be her ex-husband, and she'd be able to start her life all over again. This time, she'd go it alone because there was no way that she'd allow another man to lay one finger on her ever again.

"Tilly took June for me," she said. "And dinner isn't ready, and it's not going to be ready, because my credit card was declined at the store. We're over our limit."

"Well, shit," he grumbled, pulling a beer from the fridge, and popping off the top. "I'll put some money in the bank in the morning." She watched as Adam took a long swig of his beer and slammed the bottle down to the kitchen table, causing her to jump. "Since your sister has June, what do you say you and I have a little bit of fun, and then I'll take you out for a burger." The thought of Adam laying one finger on her repulsed her. He still smelled like the cheap hooker that he had spent the whole afternoon fucking.

"No thank you," she breathed.

"What do you mean by, 'No thank you?'" he asked.

"I mean that I don't want to have any fun with you, ever

again, Adam. It means that I know why my credit card was over the limit and I couldn't buy food for our daughter. You used my card to pay for a whore and a motel room, didn't you?" she spat.

"You watch your fucking mouth, Melody. I told you that I wasn't going to do that again, and I haven't," he said, keeping up with his lie. If given the chance, Adam would rather die than claim the truth. But she knew the truth, even if he wouldn't say it out loud. He had cheated on her before, with her best friend from high school. Yeah, that one hurt like a bitch, but she forgave him. Melody was six months pregnant and a fool for thinking that staying with Adam was better for her and her unborn child than leaving him. She should have gotten out then, but she was too afraid to make a move that would cost her the roof over her head, so she stayed, and things went from bad to worse.

After he swore that he'd give up cheating on her, he got angry. It was as if he blamed her for not allowing him to screw around. Adam started getting rough with her and after a few times pushing her around and shouting at her, he finally hit her. She took it too, not wanting to cause waves. A part of her believed that she was responsible for his anger. She could deal with his anger, it was his cheating that broke her heart, so she stayed.

But now, finding out that he had cheated again, she felt numb. Melody was ready to walk out. Her and June's bags were packed and in the trunk of her car. Tilly said that they could stay with her and her new husband, Owen, for a while until she could get back on her feet. She had a plan and for the first time in her life, Melody felt like she had some self-worth.

She defiantly raised her chin to Adam as if daring him to hit her. "You did cheat on me, Adam," she insisted. "I have the credit card records to prove it. You've been going to that motel again, and this time, you've been paying for whores. Did you really believe that I wouldn't find the charges?" she asked.

"Maybe I just didn't fucking care if you found them," he spat. Adam sucked down the rest of his beer and grabbed another one from the fridge. If he continued drinking at this pace, she only had a small window of opportunity to let him know that they were done.

"I want a divorce," she said, cutting right to the chase.

"Well, that's just too fucking bad," he shouted. "You and I are married, for better or worse, and you're not leaving me."

"I am leaving you and I'm taking June with me. I want a divorce and I'm going to go to a lawyer tomorrow. I'm sure that my credit card records will be enough to prove that you've been cheating on me." He put the new bottle of beer on the table and stepped closer to her. He smelled like cheap perfume and pussy. God, it made her want to gag, but she held it back. There was no way that she'd show any weakness around him ever again. She had already done enough of that to last a lifetime.

She stared him down and when he smiled and turned away, she thought that he was going to pick up his beer and leave her alone, but she was wrong. Adam quickly turned back and punched her so hard in the face that she landed on her ass, and damn if she didn't see stars.

"You feel better?" she slurred. She was sure that her eye would swell shut in a matter of minutes and he was only getting started—that much she knew from experience.

"Not yet, but I plan on hitting you until I do," he growled.

"That's usually your plan, asshole," she said, sitting up from the kitchen floor. He stood over her and she smiled up at him, knowing something that he didn't gave her a second wind.

"Why the fuck are you smiling at me, bitch?" he spat.

"Because for the first time, in a damn long time, I think I'm actually going to win this one," she said.

"You think that you can beat me?" he asked. Adam clenched his fist, an act that usually made her cringe, but this time she didn't feel anything. She had an ace up her sleeve—a large biker who stood in the doorway to her kitchen, and damn if he didn't look pissed off enough to tear Adam limb from limb.

"She might not be able to beat you, but I'm pretty sure that I can," Maverick growled. God, he was her knight coming to save her and she'd take it, even if she had just mentally sworn off all men forever.

"Who the fuck are you?" Adam shouted, turning his back on her. That's how he treated her—always underestimating Melody and thinking that she'd never retaliate. She was ready to take her stand, and when she found her feet grabbing the frying pan from the stove top, she swung it at the back of Adam's head, knocking him out. He fell to the kitchen floor with a thud, and she tossed the frying pan to the ground.

"Hey, Maverick," she breathed, "can you call the police for me? I need to make sure that I didn't just kill my soon-to-be ex-husband."

He shook his head at her and smiled. "I knew that I liked you, kid," he said, calling her by that annoying little nickname he used for her. Melody knelt down to find that Adam still had a pulse. She stood, not sure if that was a good or bad thing. One thing was for sure, he wouldn't let her retaliation go unpunished and there was no way that he'd underestimate her again.

MAVERICK

Maverick Blaine knew something was up when he showed up at his brother's house and found him and his new bride babysitting Melody's kid. As soon as he walked into their house, the toddler made a beeline for him and begged to be picked up. He didn't mind kids, really, and Melody's brat was the cutest one he knew. He asked her where her mama was, and she just smiled back at him, giving him that blank stare that she usually gave him as she checked him out. June was fascinated by his beard and tats. He just wished her mom felt the same way about him, but Melody was a married woman, and he wouldn't cross that line, no matter how badly he wanted to.

Mav asked Tilly where Melody was, and she told him that her sister had some things to work out with her husband. That was all he got from her before she took June from him and whisked her off to the bathroom for a bath. It wasn't until he found his brother sitting in the kitchen, drinking a beer, that he got a straight answer about what was going on. That was when Owen told him that Melody had caught her scumbag husband cheating on her, again. He couldn't believe that anyone would cheat on her once, let alone twice. Hell, the woman he knew was sassy and confident and would never let some loser cheat on her.

Owen went on to tell him that he thought that letting Melody go back to her house to face her husband alone was a bad idea. He said that the asshole liked to smack Melody around and that's when Maverick lost it. He questioned his brother for letting Melody face that jerk alone and then stormed out of the house, mumbling something about needing to beat his little brother's ass.

He was right to show up at Melody's house unannounced too. When he got there, he snuck into the back kitchen door and found her husband standing over her, shouting that he was going to beat the shit out of her. And from the looks of Melody, who was lying on the floor, he had already started. It took all his restraint not to run in and pummel the guy. And when Melody stood and hit the fucker in the back of the head with a frying pan, he felt a sense of pride that he had no right to feel about her. She was one tough chick and had had the physical and mental scars to prove it.

He called the police, and they showed up at her house, taking Melody's statement and arresting her husband for abuse. Maverick corroborated her statement, telling the cops that she acted in self-defense, and how he had found her on the floor after her husband had hit her. Mav's only regret was that Melody didn't kill the fucker. He was going to be taken to the hospital, to get checked out, and then, they were going to hold him until his bail hearing. He'd get out and then, he'd probably go after Melody and her kid, and Mav wouldn't let that happen. He just had to figure out how to convince her to let him take both her and June back to his place. Her ex would look for her at home first, and then, when he couldn't find her there, he'd head over to Tilly and Owen's place. His brother could handle the guy, but Mav didn't want Melody or June to have to go through any of that shit. Her asshole ex didn't know where he lived and that would give them both a safe haven while Melody figured out her next move.

He watched as the last of the cops left and Melody looked around her kitchen. "What now?" she asked.

"Now, we get you out of here," he said.

"Oh, yeah," she breathed. "I forgot all about calling my sister. She must be worried to death about me."

"I called Owen and filled him in. June is asleep and safe," he said, knowing that would be her next question. The few times that he was around Melody and her kid, he could tell that she was a great mother. He just had no idea that she was dealing with an abusive asshole at home.

"Thank you for doing that," she said. "God, what am I going to tell June about her father?" she asked. He really didn't have any answers for her. His own father was an asshole, and his poor mother was constantly covering for him and his bad behavior. But he and his brothers knew the deal. His father was a jerk and when he happened to be around, things were awful. Mav knew how much his mother struggled when his father would take off. She worked two jobs to put a roof over his and his brother's heads, and food on the table. The thing was, he and his brothers were so much happier when their old man was gone, and he had a feeling that June would feel the same way about her father not sticking around.

"When she's old enough, you'll tell her the truth. Tell her

how her brave mother stood up to a man who liked to beat her up. Tell her how strong her mom is, but I'm sure she'll already know all about it."

"Thank you for saying that, Mav," she whispered, swiping at the tears that were running down her cheeks. "I'm sorry I'm crying. I guess it's just been a long day. I need to get over to Tilly's. She's expecting me."

He grabbed her hand and she flinched, making him feel like a complete ass. Of course, she'd react to him that way. She had just had the shit beat out of her—Melody had the black eye to prove it. "I'm sorry," he said. "I'd never hurt you, Melody."

"I—I know that, Maverick. I'm just a little shaky is all. I didn't mean to react that way."

"I just wanted to talk to you about staying with Tilly and Owen," he said.

"Okay," she breathed, "is there a problem with me staying with them?"

"Not a problem," he said, "more like an issue. Owen is worried that after Adam gets out of jail, he'll come looking for you here."

"Right, and when he can't find me here, he'll search for me at Tilly and Owen's place. God, I'm an idiot. He doesn't want me there because he's worried that I'll put them in danger."

"No," Maverick said, "God, I'm screwing this all up. He's worried that he won't be able to protect you, Tilly, and June all by himself."

"Yeah, that makes sense," she said. "Um, I guess I'll just have to find another place for me and June to stay—you know until everything dies down with Adam." He didn't want to be the one to tell her that things might never die down with her soon-to-be ex. If he got out of jail, he might not ever leave her and June alone.

"How about you stay with me?" Maverick asked. She looked up at him as if he lost his mind, and maybe he had.

"That's not a good idea," she said. "I mean, won't I be putting you in danger then?"

He couldn't help laughing at the idea of him being put into danger by a mom and her kid staying with him. "I think that I'll be able to handle him if he shows up to my door."

"Yeah, you do seem capable," she said, looking him over. He liked the way that she took in every inch of him, letting her eyes roam his body. They had always had some unspoken connection, but he never acted on it knowing that she had a husband waiting for her at home. "But I don't want to put you out," she insisted.

"You wouldn't be putting me out at all," he assured. "I can keep you and June safe, I promise, Melody." He was making promises and getting involved—two things that he swore that he'd never do. But then again, Melody had him doing things he never thought he'd ever do, and with her, playing the protector, felt right.

MELODY

She wasn't sure what answer to give to Maverick because she was busy over analyzing her predicament. He was kind to offer to help her out, but she knew that her soon-to-be ex-husband wouldn't be behind bars forever and once Adam got out, he'd come to find her and June. He was a stubborn ass and giving up wasn't in his vocabulary.

Melody couldn't help but replay the past hour in her head as if it was on a loop. The way that the police officer looked at her as he questioned her made her feel as though she was the one at fault. "I'm guessing that you want to press charges," the police officer said, looking her over. She knew what her face probably looked like. It usually looked the same every time Adam backhanded her—bloody, and black and blue. She could feel her eye swelling shut, which was nothing new for her either.

"I would like to press charges," she said. Melody remembered looking over at Adam slumped up against the wall, holding his head.

"Yeah, well, I'd like to press charges against her," he spat in retaliation. "She attacked me with a frying pan and knocked me out. I was just defending myself."

"That's bullshit," Maverick shouted. "I watched him land the blow to her eye and was about to step in when Melody grabbed the frying pan and knocked him out. He did all that damage to her face before she retaliated. She was the one who acted in self-defense." She remembered smiling up at Mav and winced at the pain that little action caused her.

"You can both tell your side of the story as soon as you are both released from medical care. I'm assuming that they will want to keep you over night, to check for a concussion," the officer said to Adam. He turned back to Melody and looked her over. "I think you'll need to get a few stitches but will be released tonight."

"Would it be okay if I come in to give my statement tomorrow?" she asked. "I want to get back to my daughter to check on her."

"She's our daughter," Adam spat, "and I'm going to take her away from you, Melody. You'll lose everything for doing this to me."

"Shut the fuck up," Maverick shouted at Adam.

"Let's take a step back and cool down," the officer insisted. "You can go home for the night, but I'd like to see you in my office tomorrow morning at ten. Does that work for you?" he asked Melody.

"Yes, I can make that work," she agreed.

"What will happen to him?" Maverick asked, looking over at Adam.

"I'll put an officer on him while he's in the hospital, and

when he's released, I'll take him downtown and process him for spousal abuse."

"So, he'll be in jail?" Melody asked. She remembered feeling hopeful, even if it was short lived.

"For a night or two, until his arraignment. Then, it will be up to a judge to decide what happens to him next," the officer said. Melody let out her pent-up breath. She knew that they wouldn't be able to hold him forever, but she was hoping for more than a night or two.

"Do you have someplace safe to stay?" another officer asked. She looked over at Adam, who seemed to be breathlessly waiting for her to give her answer. There was no way that she'd voluntarily tell him where she and June would be staying. When Maverick made her the offer to let her and June stay with him, Adam was knocked out on the kitchen floor. Hopefully, her and June's location would stay a secret until they could go to court.

"I'd rather not say while he's here," she said, nodding to Adam. "But I'll be fine." She said it as if letting her soon-to-be ex-husband know that she wasn't going to sit around and wait for him to come for her or her daughter. There was no way that she'd ever let him touch her or June ever again.

"You won't be able to hide away forever," Adam taunted. She could tell that Maverick felt about ready to launch himself across the room to pound on Adam, but that wouldn't end well for anyone except Adam.

"Don't give him what he wants," she insisted. "He's trying to get under your skin—it's what he does. He picks the fight and that's how I end up like this," she said, pointing at her bruised face. "Don't give him that."

Maverick nodded and turned back to the officer. "Will she be going to the hospital soon?" he asked. "She shouldn't have to be around that piece of shit any longer than needed."

"The first ambulance is here, and we were going to take her husband in first since he lost consciousness," the officer said.

"Great, then get him out of here. She isn't going to answer any more questions until he's gone," Maverick insisted.

"You don't get to speak for my wife," Adam shouted as they rolled in a gurney to take him to the ambulance.

"I won't be your wife for very much longer," she insisted. "And I can speak for myself. I want him out of here," she said.

"This is my house," Adam spat as they loaded him onto the cart. "You're not even on the title. You will be the one leaving."

"Gladly," she shouted at him as they rolled him out of the back kitchen door. "I'll pack my stuff and be out of here before you are even released on bail. You won't see June again and the next time you see me is when I appear at your court case to give my statement."

"I look forward to it. See you then, honey," Adam said. She knew that this was far from over. Adam wasn't about to give up, no matter how much she threw at him, he always seemed to find a way to land on his feet.

Just remembering the conversation with the officers had her feeling exhausted all over again. She was grateful that it was over, but now, she needed to clear her head and come up with her next move. Melody sat down in the chair closest to her and sighed. "You okay?"

"No," she breathed, giving Maverick her complete honesty. "But I will be. Does that offer to stay with you still stand?" she asked.

"It does," he said. She wanted to break down and tell him

how grateful she was that he was still willing to take her and June in, but there would be time for that later.

"Great, I'm going to need some help packing up our stuff. My eye is about sealed shut. Can you give me a hand while we wait for the ambulance to get here?" she asked. The ambulance that the officers promised her never showed up, but she knew that getting checked out would not only be good for her health, but her upcoming case against Adam.

"I can run you into the emergency room to get checked out on our way back to pick up June," Maverick offered. "The cops will want to see you first thing in the morning, so you'll want to get some rest."

"You can run me by the ER, but I'll worry about all the other stuff in the morning. Right now, I just need help packing because I don't plan on coming back here again—ever." She had already started packing some of June's things earlier, while she was waiting for Adam to get home. She didn't have very much, which worked for her since she didn't want to bring much from her past with her. The faster she left her old life behind, the happier she would be.

"Fine," Maverick said, "but we better get a move on. Your eye is looking worse by the second."

"Then, we better get packing," Melody said.

"Bossy," Maverick said, smirking over at her.

"You have no idea," she said. Her sister liked to tell her that as a kid, she was the bossiest person on the planet, but all that changed when she married Adam. He seemed to beat that out of her.

She wasn't always someone who didn't stand up for herself. Before she met Adam, she was sassy and ready to defend herself to anyone who challenged her. Adam came out of nowhere, during her senior year in high school, and she allowed herself to be swept up in all the lies he fed her. He said that he'd take care of her and once they both graduated, she agreed to marry him, believing that all he wanted to do was be a good husband to her, but she was wrong. He wanted to control her, dominate her, and when she resisted, he beat her into submission. He seemed to get off on making her scream out in pain and listening to her begging him to stop. Before she even knew what was happening, she was getting beat up on the regular and unable to find her way free from Adam or the life that was strangling her to death.

Melody finished packing and Maverick drove her to the hospital. She was surprised at how calm Maverick stayed during the ride to the hospital when all she wanted to do was freak out. After a few hours of being poked and prodded, she was released and able to go back to her sister's house to pick up June. Tilly tried to convince her to stay the night since it was 2:00 in the morning, but Maverick reminded her that it was just not safe to stay with her sister and Owen. Adam would assume that she would be staying with her sister, and she couldn't put them at risk. She made a promise to her sister to check in daily and made Owen swear to keep Tilly safe as if she needed to do that. Owen adored her sister and Melody wondered if she'd ever find that same kind of devotion in a man. Maybe she had blown her shot by marrying so young. She didn't really know what she was getting into, and Adam turned out to be an abusive asshole. Melody was sure that she didn't deserve another shot and that was on her. Right now, she needed to concentrate on raising her daughter, and the rest could wait to be worried over on another day.

Maverick helped her gather up June's things and get her daughter into the car seat that he had installed in the back seat of his pickup truck. He insisted that they leave her car behind because it could be easily traced since Adam owned it. He owned everything and rebuilding her life from scratch wasn't going to be easy, but she planned on doing just that—if not for herself, then for her daughter.

By the time he got them back to his house, Melody felt about ready to drop. Maverick gave her a quick tour of his home and settled her and June in his spare room. "Are you sure you wouldn't be more comfortable putting June in her own bed?" he asked. "I have another spare room right next door."

"I'm sure," she said. "I have a feeling that she'll wake up in the middle of the night and I don't want her to be scared that she's in a strange place. Plus, I'd hate for her to wake you up crying. You look as tired as I feel," she said.

"I am tired, but you shouldn't worry about me," he insisted. "I'll be fine with whatever you decide." Melody felt bad that she was invading his space with a toddler in tow. She didn't want to be a burden, but she was sure that they were just that for the big biker.

"I appreciate that, but for the first few nights, I feel this sleeping arrangement might be for the best. Once she gets to know you and this place a little better, I might just take you up on your offer." He nodded and started out of the room.

"If you need me, I'm just across the hallway," he offered.

"Thank you," she almost whispered. She wanted to tell him that there was no way that she was going to need him or step one foot into his bedroom, but she left that part unsaid.

"Mommy," June whimpered as she covered her daughter with the blankets on the bed.

"I'm here, honey," Melody said.

"In my bed?" her daughter asked. June started talking at a young age and Melody had forgotten what it was like to have a baby around. But right now, her daughter looked so tiny and fragile. She just hoped like hell that she'd be able to keep her safe and as far away from Adam as possible.

"Yep, I'm in your bed," Melody said. "I'm going to sleep with you tonight." The toddler smiled and gave a half-hearted cheer.

"Daddy too?" the little girl asked.

"No, Daddy won't be sleeping with us tonight. He had to go away for a little bit, so we're staying with one of Mommy's friends." Could she call Maverick that? Was he really one of her friends? June seemed to like him, from what little she knew about him, and Melody had to admit, she more than liked the big guy. Every time she saw him, she felt this unwavering pull to him that she just couldn't explain. Of course, she ignored it since she was married to Adam. Making her marriage work for the sake of her daughter had become her top priority, but now, she'd have nothing standing in her way when she felt those damn butterflies in her tummy whenever Maverick so much as looked in her direction.

"I want Daddy," her daughter cried. Despite all his bad qualities, Adam was a decent father and seemed to love June. Maybe her sister was right, and it was only a matter of time before he'd go after their daughter and beat her as he did Melody, but so far, she was his favorite punching bag.

"I know you do, honey, but Daddy did something bad and he needs to go away for a little bit," Melody said. How the hell she was going to explain all this to her daughter was beyond her. Maybe she should stick to the basics while she was little, but sooner or later, June was going to grow up and start asking her some questions. They would be hard to answer but she'd find a way to navigate her way through them and answer her daughter honestly.

Her daughter quietly sobbed and then stuck her thumb into her mouth. It was her go-to move to self-soothe. Melody smiled, pushing her daughter's hair back from her sweet face. "That's right, honey, just close your eyes and try to sleep." June sucked her thumb for a few minutes as Melody stroked her head and finally gave up the fight, letting her eyes close as she drifted off to sleep. Melody gently kissed her daughter's head and winced at the pain it caused.

"Tylenol," she whispered to herself. Melody gently extricated herself from the covers and climbed out of bed, noting every ache she felt in her body. She was ready to fall into bed but knew that it would be pointless to try to sleep without some painkillers.

She padded down to the kitchen and turned on the light. "You okay?" Maverick asked from behind her, making her jump.

"Jesus, you scared the hell out of me, Maverick," she squeaked.

"Sorry, I just heard you coming down the stairs and I wanted to check on you," he admitted. "Is June okay? I heard her crying."

"Oh God," she breathed. This was exactly what she was trying to avoid. "I'm so sorry," she said. "I'll try to keep her as quiet as possible from now on."

He barked out his laugh, making her jump again. Everything about the man was big and loud—something that she would likely never get used to. "Good luck with that," he said. "The one thing that I know about kids is that the one thing that they aren't is quiet."

She giggled, "You're right about that," she said. "But all the same, I'm going to try to keep her as quiet as humanly possible."

"That really isn't necessary, but I appreciate the offer," he said. "Are you hungry?" he asked. She was starving since she had skipped dinner to get the shit beat out of her by her husband after accusing him of cheating on her.

"I am, but I actually came down for some Tylenol," she said. "My head and face are throbbing."

He winced, looking her face over. She was sure that she looked dreadful. The doctor at the ER had to give her five stitches for her split lip and her eye was swollen shut. "I bet," he said. "You sit and I'll grab the Tylenol and some ice for you. Then, I'll make you some soup. That should be easy enough to eat with your split lip."

"You don't have to go to all that trouble," she said. "I can do it."

"No need," he said, "I don't have house guests very often and like to take care of people. My mother used to say that I was the classic oldest child, although I am a twin, so I guess I have competition for that title. I like to fix problems and take care of everyone. I'm also bossy, but you pointed out that you are too, and maybe we should leave that roll to you while you're staying here."

"I'm sure that there is room for two bossy people under one roof," she said. "So, you don't have house guests very often?" she asked. Melody wasn't sure why it made her a little bit giddy that he didn't have women over very often.

"Nope, I'm kind of a loner, and bringing anyone back here seemed like more of a complication than it was worth," he said.

"What about a girlfriend?" she asked as Maverick handed her two Tylenol and a glass of water. Melody took one pill at a time, careful not to dribble any of the water from her busted lip. She was unsuccessful and gently wiped away the water from her chin before taking the second pill.

"No girlfriend," he said. She felt those same butterflies as she usually did whenever Maverick was in the same room with her and she rubbed her tummy, trying to calm them. "At least, no long-term girlfriend. I'm not the type of guy who likes to get tangled up with a woman." He handed her an ice pack that he pulled out from his freezer, and she nodded her thanks as she gently held it to her aching eye.

"So, you're gay then," she grumbled. To think that she had been feeling butterflies at just the sight of him and Maverick turned out to be into guys. "Not that there is anything wrong with that," she quickly added.

"Thanks for that, but I'm not gay," he insisted.

"But you just said that you don't like to get tangled up with women," she reminded.

He rolled his eyes at her as he pulled a can of soup from his cabinet. "Is chicken noodle good?" he asked.

"Yes," she said, hoping that he'd get back to their conversation.

"I meant that I don't have time for messy relationships," he said. "I'm not the kind of guy who does well with clingy women," he admitted. Her heart sank. If Maverick didn't do relationships, that meant that he just liked to hook up and she didn't have the kind of lifestyle that permitted that. She had a daughter to think about. Hell, she still had a husband to get rid of before she could even think about butterflies and all the other shit that Maverick made her feel. She wasn't sure why she was upset—she had no right to be, but she was sad that Maverick didn't do relationships.

"Yeah well, I'm not sure that I'll ever want another relationship with a man, so we at least agree on that point," she whispered.

"Not all men act like your husband," Maverick said. "Real men don't hit women. Hell, I'd never lay a finger on you, Melody," he admitted.

"Noted," she said under her breath. She was getting his message loud and clear—Maverick didn't want a relationship with her or any other woman, for that matter. And, for some reason, he found her so repulsive, that he'd never even lay a finger on her. Yeah, she got the message—Maverick didn't seem to feel the same attraction that she felt to him, and that was good to know. Now, she wouldn't go and make a fool of herself for a man she had no business wanting.

MAVERICK

He had to go into the bar for church, and telling Mace that he wasn't going to be there wasn't an option, especially since Melody's husband had been released on bail earlier that morning. His club's Prez wasn't the kind of guy who liked to take no for an answer. The problem was, that he couldn't leave Melody and June all alone at his place, and taking them with him wasn't an option either. Calling his twin brother for help was probably a huge mistake, but he had no other choice.

He pulled his cell from his pocket and dialed Steel's number. "This better be good," Steel answered, "I was sleeping."

"Sorry to wake you, but I need a favor," Maverick said.

"And if I remember correctly, you actually are the one who owes me a favor," Steel grumbled. His brother had covered a meeting for him with a new security client. Owen had booked him without asking his schedule and he couldn't make the appointment and finish working on the bike that he had promised to get done for a customer, so he had Steel pretend to be him and it all worked out. They were identical twins, although most people could tell them apart by their tattoos and well, attitudes. Maverick was considered the easy-go-lucky one of the pair, and that always made him chuckle given the fact that he hated most people.

"Okay, so now, I'll owe you two," Maverick promised. He knew that Steel wouldn't collect. He hated asking anyone for help—even his brothers. "Come on, just help me out, Steel."

"Fine," Steel agreed. "But for the record, I'm not someone who's just going to jump every time you call me."

"Noted," Maverick said.

"What's the favor?" Steel asked.

"I need you to babysit for me," Maverick said. "I have to go down to the club for a Road Reapers meeting, and I don't want to leave Melody or June alone here."

"Right, Owen kind of filled me in on what's going on," Steel said. "You've taken in Tilly's sister and her kid."

"I have," Maverick said. "They needed a place to lay low until we can get her husband put away for what he's done to her."

"Yeah, I heard that her husband is a real asshole," Steel said.

"Any man who beats a woman like that is an ass," Maverick agreed. "So, you'll do it?"

"I'll do it," Steel agreed. "What time should I get there?"

"How about seven? Melody isn't going to like this very much, but it's the only way that I can get down to the bar to find out what Mace wants. Do you have any idea why he's summonsed me to church tonight? It's like he's issued me a private invitation or something."

"Nope," Steel said. "I have no idea. I let him know that I

wasn't going to be able to make it because I planned on finding a woman to have some fun with."

"You didn't tell him that though, did you?" Maverick asked. Mace wouldn't have let Steel out of their meeting for a night of hot sex with a random woman he picked up.

"Of course, I didn't," Steel admitted. "I'm not a fool. But now, I'm going to be babysitting your woman."

"Jesus, she's not my woman, and if Tilly heard you say something like that, she'd kick your ass," Maverick said. Their new sister-in-law was a force to be reckoned with. "I told you that I'm just helping her sister and niece out while her husband is out on bail."

"Has he gotten out yet?" Steel asked.

"He got out this morning, but we were expecting it. They can't hold him forever, but his day in court will come and when it does, they will toss him in a cage and throw away the key," Maverick growled. That was the plan, at least.

"And if they don't?" Steel asked.

"What does that mean?" Maverick asked.

"If her husband doesn't end up in prison, what happens then?" Maverick hadn't really given that much thought. He wasn't a fool, he knew that it was an option, but he hoped that it wouldn't happen.

"I guess we'll figure that out when and if it happens," Maverick said. "So, we're good for tonight?" he asked, wanting to change the topic.

"I'll see you at seven," Steel said, ending the call. Maverick shoved his cell phone back into his pocket and turned to find Melody standing in the doorway to his bedroom.

"Did you seriously just get me a babysitter?" she asked.

Maverick winced, "You heard that, huh?" There would be no denying his conversation with Steel.

"What the hell were you thinking? I'm a mother. I'm the one who hires a sitter, not someone who needs a sitter," she shouted.

"I get that, but I promised to keep you and June safe, and I have to go out tonight," he admitted.

"Out?" she asked. "Are you ditching us for a woman? Did you get a booty call, and you can't pass it up?" He couldn't hide his smile and when she seemed to get even madder, he barked out his laugh, causing Melody to cross her arms over her chest. God, she was adorable when she got mad. But the last man she was angry with ended up on the kitchen floor after she had knocked him out with a frying pan.

"Adam just got out of jail, and he'll be looking for you," Maverick explained.

"I'm aware," she spat. "Are you going to tell me where you're going?" He wanted to tell her that it wasn't any of her business, but from the look on her face, she wasn't going to accept that answer.

"I'm going into the bar," he said.

"To meet a woman?" she asked.

"No, to meet with my club's Prez. Mace has called a meeting and I'm being summonsed. I can't tell him no," Maverick said. "And I can't leave you and June here alone, so I called my twin brother, Steel."

"I met him at Tilly and Owen's wedding," she said. "He looks exactly like you." Owen and Tilly had a small ceremony at the courthouse with family and a few of the guys from the club. Then, they all went back to the bar for a makeshift party to celebrate. Maverick was happy that Steel showed up for Owen's special day.

"Right," Maverick agreed, "but, he's not me." It hurt his feelings a bit that she couldn't see the difference between him and Steel.

"Well, I know that," she said. "He's your twin."

"He is, and he's going to hang out with you and June until I can get back," he said.

"And I don't have a say in any of this?" she asked.

"No, you don't," he said. "Just let me do my job and keep you both safe."

"Fine, I didn't know that I was just a job," she sassed. Melody wasn't about to make any of this any easier on him. She turned to walk out of the room and as if on cue, June started crying for her.

"Melody," he called after her.

"Can't talk now, Mav. June needs me and I have a job to do." Yeah, maybe he deserved that, but it still stung. All he could do was watch Melody make her way down the narrow hallway to the room that she and June shared. She was definitely going to give him trouble around every corner and a part of him liked that she was a challenge. It meant that she was a fighter, and that was exactly what Melody was going to have to do if she wanted to beat her husband in court.

Maverick hated leaving Melody, but he knew that she was in good hands with his brother. He just hoped like hell that his brother kept his hands to himself. When Mav was about to leave, Steel asked again if there was anything between him and Melody and he almost lied and told his brother that there was.

He didn't like the way that Steel was looking at her or the fact that Melody seemed so comfortable around his twin.

He walked into the back of the bar, hoping to slip in early, talk to Mace, and then go back home and kick his brother to the curb. "You came," Mace said, standing in the back of the empty barroom.

"Well, you summonsed me, so I thought that me showing up wasn't an option," Maverick grumbled.

"It wasn't an option," Mace said. "Follow me to my office. I have something that you might be interested in seeing."

"Shit, that doesn't sound good," Maverick said.

"It's not," Mace said back over his shoulder. Maverick followed him back to his office and sat down on the couch. Mace turned on the television and pulled up the security feed from the bar's parking lot. Maverick and Owen had installed the security cameras and system for the bar, so he knew exactly what he was looking at.

Mace fast-forwarded about two hours in, and Maverick didn't hide his gasp when he saw Adam snooping around the back of the bar. "Fuck," he spat. "How did he know to look around here?"

"I guess he figured out that you're a part of the Road Reapers and that you are taking care of his wife. You were there when they arrested the guy, right? I mean, that's what Owen told me when I showed him this footage."

"Yeah," Maverick said. "And my brother should have filled me in about this before I came down here. If he knows that I have his wife, then he will figure out where I live and now that I've left her, I'm giving him the opening he might be looking for."

"Did you leave her all alone?" Mace asked.

"Of course not," Maverick growled, "I've called in a favor with Steel and he's babysitting her."

"Is that a good idea?" Mace asked. "You know, having your twin brother watch your woman?"

"Why does everyone keep calling her that? She's not my woman," he said. They had only known each other a short time now, and sure, she had been living under his roof since her husband attacked her last week, but that didn't make her his woman, even if he wanted her to be.

Mace barked out his laugh, "Sure, man," he said. "You keep telling yourself that. I have eyes and could see how upset you were to find her husband snooping around outside. You wouldn't get that upset if she was just some woman you didn't care about." He had a point. Maverick did care about Melody, but he thought that her attraction to her was because he knew that she was off limits. He seemed to always want what he couldn't have. But now that Melody was free of her abusive husband, did that change things? He still felt like a teenager every time she walked into the room, and he had taken more cold showers than he cared to admit since she had moved in. Yeah, maybe he did want her to be his woman, but she wasn't. Not yet at least.

"Just because I got upset that her ex is snooping around here, doesn't make her my woman. She's been through a lot and I'm helping her out. She's my sister-in-law's sister and that means she's family." Maverick insisted.

"Okay, don't get all worked up man," Mace said, "I believe you. So, do you want me to put a few extra guys on your place? You know, watch you around the clock, just to be on the safe side."

"That would be great, man," Maverick said. "I'd appreciate that. I'll give Owen a call too and I'm sure that he and Steel will help keep an eye on things." He was going to have a little talk with Owen first about keeping information from him, but then, he was sure that his brother would help out to keep Melody and June safe.

"Done, now get out of here," Mace ordered. "You need to relieve Steel from his babysitting gig and figure out how to deal with your feelings about your new roommate."

"Shut the fuck up," Maverick grumbled on his way out of the office. "Thanks for not making me stay for church."

"Don't worry, you'll pay for it in the future, when all this shit is over," Mace said.

"Got it," Maverick said. "Thanks for everything, man. I mean that." He was sure that the extra manpower was going to be necessary since Melody's husband didn't seem like the type of guy who was going to just give up.

MELODY

She had to admit, Steel was fun to hang out with, but she missed Maverick. It was the first time that he had left her in a week, and she was surprised at how that made her feel. She had popped some popcorn after settling June down to sleep and cuddled under a throw blanket on the sofa. For a big, bad biker, Maverick seemed to have a flare for decorating. His home was cozy and felt like someplace where she could spend some time, even if she wasn't being forced to. That's what this time at his place was beginning to feel like to her. June kept crying that she wanted to go home, and she wasn't sure how to tell her toddler that they had no home to go back to anymore. There was no way that she'd take her daughter back to her old house knowing that Adam would probably be there waiting for them. When this mess was over, she'd find a way to give June the kind of home she deserved. Melody would make sure that her daughter was safe, no matter what she had to do to make that happen.

"Can I join you?" Steel asked. She nodded to the seat next to her, continuing to eat her popcorn. "Late-night snack?"

"Yeah, I didn't really eat much at dinner tonight," she admitted. June was fussier than usual and refused to eat her food, so Melody had spent most of her time coaxing her daughter to eat. Maverick didn't seem to mind the fuss, but she didn't want to become a thorn in his side. Sooner or later, he was going to get sick of her daughter's outbursts and kick them both to the curb.

"You don't talk much, do you?" Steel asked. It usually took her awhile to warm up to people before she became chatty. Steel might look like Maverick, but he wasn't him and she didn't know how much she could say in front of him.

"If I have something to say, I say it," she said, "but, I really have nothing to say right now. Why, did you have something that you wanted to talk about?" she asked.

"Um, sure how about you and my brother," he said.

"What about me and your brother?" she asked. Melody had a pretty good idea of what Steel was hinting at, but she wanted to make him say the words.

"Well, you two seem cozy and all. I mean, you're living here, right?" Steel asked.

"He's letting me stay here because my husband, well, soon-to-be ex-husband, attacked me again and this time, I pressed charges. He's probably pissed off after his release from jail and looking for me to have his revenge. I won't let that happen to me or my daughter. When Mav asked me to stay here with him, I agreed because honestly, I had nowhere else to go. If I ended up at my sister's place, Owen would have his hands full if Adam showed up there, he might not be able to keep all of us safe."

"I get that," Steel said. "Owen's top-notch at what he does, but he'd be worried about you three and might lose focus.

Maverick moving you in here was a good idea. I'm just wondering if you didn't agree to move in here for other reasons than safety." She wanted to scoff at his suggestion, but he was partially right. She was attracted to Maverick and the thought of moving into his place did make her feel like a giddy schoolgirl, not that she was about to admit that to his twin brother. If she was going to tell anyone that truth, it would be Maverick. She just had to get up the nerve to get the words out and she wasn't sure that would happen anytime soon.

"If that's true, then it's none of your business, is it?" she questioned.

"My brother is my business. He and Owen are the only people on this planet who matter to me. So, if you are here to screw with his feelings, then I'm warning you, you'll have to answer to me."

She smiled over at Steel, loving the way that he stuck up for his brother. She admired him for it. She would have done the same for her sister. "I like you, Steel," she said. "But I can assure you that I'm not here to hurt your brother and I'm not sure that I even have the power you're implying that I do. I can't hurt his feelings because your brother doesn't feel anything for me. He's doing this to be kind. He considers me family because Tilly is married to your brother. Heck, I guess that does make us family."

"It does," Steel agreed, "but, I can promise you that I don't feel the same way about you that my brother does. He has feelings for you, Melody, and they have nothing to do with your sister being married to our little brother." Was Steel right? Did Mav have feelings for her? That was impossible. He didn't give her any indication that he liked her in any way other than a friend. He had even mentioned that she was hands-off since she was married, not that she understood what he meant by that at the time.

"Well, we will just have to agree to disagree," she sassed.

"What the hell does that mean?" he growled. He sounded just as grumpy as Maverick did when she disagreed with him. She almost wanted to giggle, but she knew from dealing with Mav that was never a good idea unless she wanted to piss him off further.

"It means that I don't agree with your assessment about how Maverick feels about me. So, we'll have to agree to disagree because I'm probably not going to change your mind and you won't change mine," she insisted.

"I don't have to prove that I'm right to you. I'm sure that my brother will do that for me in no time. I could tell that leaving you was painful for him and if he thinks that I'm interested in you, which he does, he'll lose his mind being jealous. Well, until he finally breaks down and tells you how he feels about you," Steel said.

"Why would he think that you're interested in me?" she asked Steel.

"Because I hinted to the fact that I was," he said, smirk firmly in place.

"But you don't even know me. I mean, we met for a brief few minutes at my sister's wedding, but then you took off. How can you be interested in me?" she asked.

Steel shrugged, "I'm not," he admitted. "But I like fucking around with my twin brother. Watching Maverick squirm is one of my favorite hobbies. It always has been."

"You're kind of an ass," she said, laughing to herself.

"Yep," he boasted, "but, can you sit there and tell me that you haven't ever done the same to your sister?" he asked. She was married and pregnant by the time her sister graduated from high school. Her sister had always been one of her best friends, and screwing around with her feelings wasn't something that Melody had ever thought about doing to Tilly.

"Never," she admitted. "My sister and I have always been close. I never thought about fucking around with her feelings."

Steel's smile was back in place, and he nodded. "I knew you were a good person, Melody, but you're a fucking saint."

She barked out her laugh and shook her head, "No, I'm not," she insisted. "Remember, I knocked my husband out with a frying pan."

"And you had good reason. He did that to your face right?" Steel asked, looking over her faded bruises. She still looked a bit gnarly, and even had stitches in her upper lip for a couple more days. Her eye wasn't completely sealed shut, but she could barely see out of it, and it was now an interesting shade of purple. The bruises were extensive and hard to cover, so she stopped trying. Steel was seeing her husband's handy work in all its glory.

"Yes, he did this to me," she said, holding her hand up to her face as if framing it for viewing. "But I won't let him do it again to me, ever. That's why I'm here and it doesn't matter how Maverick feels about me. I'll always be grateful to him for taking June and me in."

"You don't ever have to thank me for that," Maverick said from the kitchen doorway.

"How long have you been standing there?" she squeaked. For such a big guy, he moved like a ninja.

"Long enough," he said. "Let me talk to Steel for a second, and then, you and I should talk." She nodded, not sure if she should ask the million questions now running through her head —the first being if they were going to talk about feelings. She wasn't sure if she could handle that if they were, but she was going to be honest with him. Melody owed Mav at least that much.

Steel followed his brother into the kitchen, turning back to smile at her. "It was nice getting to know you, Melody," he said. "Anytime you need to be babysat in the future, just have Mav give me a call." He winked at her, causing her to giggle again and she waved at him as he turned to follow his brother out of the room.

Melody couldn't really make out their voices. She sat as quietly as possible, trying to hear what they were saying, but she could only hear their whispers. One thing she was sure of—they were talking about her. She had heard her name quite a few times and if she wasn't mistaken, she had heard Adam's too.

As soon as the backdoor shut, she pretended to be interested in the television program She was watching, on mute, and eating handfuls of popcorn. Melody hoped it was enough to throw Maverick off so that he wouldn't guess that she was trying to eavesdrop.

"Steel left," he said, sitting down next to her on the couch in the same spot that his brother had just vacated. She nodded, not really taking her eyes off the television. "I'd like to talk." What was it about these two wanting to talk to her?

"Steel was chatty too," she said. "What would you like to talk about Mav?" she asked.

"My brother was chatty?" he asked. "Steel really isn't a talker."

"Well, he talked my ear off," she countered. "So, what can I do for you, Mav?" She was beginning to think that she wasn't going to like the conversation that Maverick wanted to have with her.

"What did you and my brother talk about?" he asked.

"You are not going to let this go, are you?" she asked.

"No, I want to know what you and my brother talked about," he said.

"Fine, your brother asked me if I have feelings for you and if that was why I was staying here with you," she admitted.

"And what did you tell him?" Maverick asked.

"I told Steel that it was none of his business," she said.

Maverick threw back his head and laughed. "I bet he loved that."

"He did not, but then, he followed up by telling me that you have feelings for me." Maverick sobered and she wondered if she had hit on something. Maybe she had and that's why he looked like a deer caught in the headlights. "Do you have feelings for me, Mav?" she boldly asked.

"That fucker," he grumbled.

"That's not an answer to my question, is it?" she challenged.

"No, it's not," he said, "but, I'm not sure that you'll like my answer."

"How about you try me?" she asked.

"Okay, let's just say that my brother wasn't wrong about how I feel about you," Maverick admitted.

"So then, you do have feelings for me," she said.

"I've had feelings for you since the day that I showed up at your house to tell you that your sister was attacked and in the hospital." Mav showed up at her house to tell her that Tilly was attacked at the bar that housed his club, by her now ex-boss. She had stolen a thumb drive from her boss to prove that he was doing something illegal, she just wasn't sure what she was about to get herself into. Tilly was always one to do the right thing, but she was in over her head. When she was released from the hospital, she went back to Owen's house and that was when their love story started.

"You can't be serious," she insisted. "You didn't know me then. Heck, for all you knew, I was happily married with a kid."

"I know that, but when I saw you for the first time, all I could think was, 'Just breathe'. You took my breath away, honey, and made my heart feel like it was going to beat out of my chest. I felt something for you from the start, honey," Maverick admitted.

"Oh," she breathed as he slid closer to her. "I'm not sure what to say now."

"Tell me that I'm not alone in how I feel about you, Melody. Say that you at least feel something for me," he begged. She thought about keeping her feelings to herself, but that wouldn't be fair to him. She owed Maverick the truth, and she was going to have to find the courage to tell him.

"I have feelings for you too," she admitted. "I kind of brushed it off when we first met. I told myself that you were just a good-looking guy who took my breath away."

"I did?" he asked, puffing his chest out, making her giggle.

"You did, and when Adam got home that night, he reminded me that I wasn't worth anything to anyone, and I pushed those feelings down because I never thought that you'd feel the same way about me."

He pulled her to his lap, and she willingly let him. "So, you think that I'm good-looking?" he asked.

"Don't get a swelled head, but I do," she said. "But the thing that drew me to you was how kind you are."

"Great, well, let's not let that get around at the club. I can't have my brothers thinking that I'm kind and that's why women want me."

"Wait—what do you mean by women?" she asked.

"It was just a figure of speech," he said. "I've already told you that I don't bring back women to my place, and I don't date."

"Well, then, what are you planning on doing with me, Mav?" she asked.

"I plan on taking you up to my room and making you mine," he whispered into her ear, making her shiver. "But once I do that, there will be no going back, honey. Are you up for that?"

"For being yours?" she asked. He nodded. "Yes, I'd like to be yours, Maverick."

"Good," he breathed, pulling her into his arms and standing with her. She wrapped her arms around his neck as he cradled her against his chest. Melody was sure that he was going to make good on his promise and she had to admit, she was looking forward to everything he planned on doing with her.

MAVERICK

Maverick carried her up to his bed, laying her across it. He didn't want to ask this next question, but it was out before he could stop the words. "Are you sure that this is what you want, honey?" he asked. He feared that she was going to tell him that she didn't want him, but from the way she looked him over, and then reached for him, he knew that she hadn't changed her mind.

"I'm sure," she said. "I want this, Maverick. I want you." He tugged off his t-shirt and climbed onto the bed next to her. He couldn't get enough of her as he kissed his way up and down her body. Her hands were all over his chest and when she reached down to undo the button to his jeans, he nearly swallowed his damn tongue.

"Let's hold off on that for a minute," he said, pulling her hands into his own.

"Have you changed your mind, Mav?" she breathed.

"Not a chance in hell," he said.

"Good, then how about you let me get you naked?" she asked.

"It's been a while since I've done this. I've had kind of a dry spell, honey," he said.

"How long of a dry spell?" she asked. He rubbed her hands into his own, noting how small and soft they were against his hard, calloused ones. Working on bikes had left him with more calluses than he liked, but his work was honest, and it paid the bills.

"I haven't had a woman for about six months, and if you get me naked, this will go a whole lot faster than either of us would like. How about you let me take my time and take care of you, first. Then, you can get me naked and have your way with me," he teased.

"Well, if you insist," she said, releasing his hands and laying back to give him full access to her body. He looked her over as if trying to decide where to begin. "Do your worst," she teased.

"I'm going to make you regret those words, honey," he growled, tugging her shirt over her head, and her pants down her legs, leaving her laying bare next to him. He loved the moan that she gave him as he ran his hands over her taut nipples. She was so responsive to his every touch; he was sure that he wouldn't be able to hold out very long once he got inside of her.

Maverick spread her legs and settled between them as Melody moaned out his name. "I love how loud you are, baby," he said.

"Oh, God," she whispered. "Am I being loud? I don't want to wake up June."

"I'm sure she's sound asleep," he assured. "Just relax, honey, I've got you." She laid her head back, giving him the green light to proceed. "Good girl," he growled as he dipped his head to lick through her folds. "You smell and taste good, baby," he praised.

"Maverick," she moaned his name again. "When you talk to me like that, it makes me hot."

"You like dirty talk?" he asked.

"I guess I do," she whimpered.

"You guess?" he asked.

"Yeah, Adam never did any of this for me," she admitted.

"He never talked dirty to you?" Mav asked. Maybe it was unconventional to talk about her ex when they were in the middle of having sex, but he wanted to know what she liked and didn't like while she was in his bed.

"No, and he never did what you're about to do to me either," she whispered as if telling him a secret.

"He never went down on you?" Maverick asked. It was one of his favorite things to do to please a woman. He had been told that he was quite good at it, too, not that he wanted to brag.

"No," she breathed.

"Do you want me to eat your pussy, honey?" he asked. Maverick was lazily running his fingers through her drenched folds and from the new wetness that coated her pussy, he could tell that she wanted him to do exactly that.

"Yes," she moaned. He dipped his head and sucked her clit into his mouth, and she nearly bucked them both off the bed.

"Hold still, honey, and I'll make you feel good," he promised. She pulled the sheets into her hands as if needing to get a grip before he went on giving her what she asked him for. He chuckled and dipped his head to lick through her folds again. When he finally finished with her, Melody was completely rung out from shouting his name as she rode his face, finding not just one, but four orgasms.

He stood and grabbed her legs, pulling her limp body to the edge of the bed. "My turn," he growled. Maverick unbuttoned his jeans and let them fall to the floor as he palmed his erection. Her eyes on every move that his hands made had him just about coming before he even got inside of her.

"You ready?" he asked.

"Yes," she breathed. "I want you, Mav. I want all of you." She reached for him, and he didn't make her wait. He filled her body, pulling Melody into his arms. God, she felt right there. It was something that he never thought he find with any woman—someone who felt like home when he held her.

"You're so fucking perfect," he whispered into her ear as he pumped in and out of her body.

"You are too, Mav," she breathed. He waited for her to find her release and when she cried out his name again, he quickly followed her over, pumping into her body a few more times, losing himself inside of her.

"Fucking perfect," he whispered as they collapsed onto the bed together.

She cuddled in against his body and yawned. "Can I spend the night here?" she asked.

"I plan on you being in my bed every night from here on out," he said. "You good with that?"

"What about June?" she asked.

"We will make sure that she's good, but I want you with me, honey." He wanted her in his bed, naked, pressed up against his body just like she was now.

"I'm good with that, as long as June is okay, I'd like to sleep in your bed. I like being yours, Mav." Hearing her say that made his heart feel like it might beat out of his chest again.

"I like hearing you say that," he said.

She yawned again, "How about we get some sleep? My daughter gets up early and I'm worn out."

"Before you sleep, I have something that I need to tell you," he said. Maverick knew that she wasn't going to like what he was about to tell her, but he had no choice. Melody had a right to know what was going on with her husband.

"Okay, that sounds serious," she said, sitting up in bed.

"It is, and I hate telling you this now, but Adam was snooping around the bar last night. He was caught on the surveillance camera and that's why Mace called me down there tonight."

"Did you have any idea why he wanted to talk to you?" she asked.

"No, I thought that he wanted me at the meeting or something. He wanted to show me the video and ask if I wanted him to post a few guys around my house. I agreed to have the extra help, but if your husband has figured out that you're with me, he'll eventually find you here and we'll need a plan."

"I hate that he's still my husband. I called a lawyer today and set up a meeting to process the paperwork to start divorce proceedings. He told me that I should have no problem given that I've pressed charges against Adam and that I have a restraining order against him now. But it's still a process and will take some time."

"Everything worth waiting for takes time, honey. And you're worth waiting for," he said.

"Thank you for saying that, Mav," she said. "For so long now, I believed everything that Adam told me to be true. He loved to put me down and belittle me at every turn. He told me that I was a bad mother and that I was a worthless wife. It just took me some time to decide that he was wrong and that I didn't need to listen to him anymore. Hell, his cheating on me again was a good thing."

Maverick couldn't imagine ever wanting to cheat on Melody. No other woman could compare to her. "How so?" he asked.

"His cheating finally gave me the gumption to stand up to him and demand a divorce. I guess it was my last straw." He wondered how Adam beating her up wasn't the last straw, but that wasn't something he wanted to ask her about now.

"I think it might be good for you to get some help," he whispered. "You know, go talk to someone about everything that you've been through. It has to have taken a toll."

"I'll think about it," she whispered. "It's still so fresh, I just need some time."

"Take the time that you need, honey, but talking to someone might be good for you." She nodded and Maverick knew not to push it any further. He couldn't force her to talk to someone if she didn't want to.

"What are we going to do about Adam snooping around your club?" she asked.

"Well, the guys are keeping an eye on the place right now, taking shifts, and tomorrow morning, Owen and Steel are going to come back over to see if we can beef up security around here."

"Right, but you already have good security," she reminded. "And if Adam wants to get to me and June, he'll find a way." She was right, and that sucked. He wouldn't sugar coat the truth for her.

"You're right," he agreed. "But I'm going to do everything in my power to make sure that he can't get to either of you. Do you trust me, Melody?" he asked.

"With my and June's lives," she said. That was a lot of pressure, but he was up for the challenge.

"Good, then we have a plan," he said.

"What?" She asked. "When did we come up with a plan?"

"Well, you said that you trust me, and I plan on keeping you and June safe. That's the plan," he insisted.

Melody giggled, "If that's what you want to call it," she said. "At best, it's an idea, but we can call it a plan if you want to."

"Thanks," he grumbled. He tugged her into his body again and loved the way that she snuggled into him. For some damn reason, it felt right to have her by his side. Maverick took a chance tonight, telling Melody how he felt about her, and it had paid off in spades. He was lucky enough to get the girl, and now, he just had to figure out how to keep her and her daughter safe from her soon-to-be ex-husband.

MELODY

Melody woke to an empty bed and rolled over to stretch, groaning at the muscles that ached. It wasn't a bad ache—more of a delicious ache from being used by Maverick a few times during the night. He didn't let her get much sleep, and that was fine by her because Mav gave her more love and attention than she had felt in a long time. In fact, she couldn't ever remember Adam loving her that way. Her husband was more concerned about himself and getting what he needed from her, but Maverick was different. He asked her if she was with him every step along the way and God, was she with him.

She got up and pulled on Mav's t-shirt that she found on the floor and padded down the hallway to check on June. Her daughter wasn't in her bed, and she panicked as she ran through the house looking for her. Melody found June sitting on Maverick's lap as she ate pancakes with Owen and Steele on either side of them.

"You should have told me she was up," Melody scolded.

"I thought you might need some extra sleep," he said, smiling over at her and even giving her an outrageous wink. Owen and Steel looked her over as she tried to tug her t-shirt down her legs.

"Um, if you have her, I'm going to grab a quick shower," she said, suddenly feeling very underdressed.

"We're good," Maverick assured. "You have your shower and take your time."

"Thank you," she squeaked, turning to leave the room. She wasn't sure how she was going to explain any of this to her sister, but she was sure that she had to get to Tilly before Owen told her. Her sister would kill her if she didn't tell her that she slept with Maverick.

Melody took a quick shower and pulled on some clean sweats, making sure that every inch of her body was now covered. She was ready to face her brother-in-law and Steel, but first, she was going to call Tilly and give her a quick explanation.

It was now or never. Melody pulled her cell from the night-stand and dialed her sister's number. "Hey, is everything okay over there?" Tilly asked. "I know that the three of them together can be a lot, but they're just trying to help you and June."

"I know that," Melody insisted. "I just have something that I need to tell you and I think you should hear it from me and not Owen."

"Okay, you sound like I should be sitting down for this," Tilly said.

Melody shrugged, knowing that her sister couldn't see her. "Maybe you should sit down," she said. "You might not like what I'm about to tell you."

"Oh, God," her sister breathed. "I thought that you said that you guys are okay."

"We are. I'm good and so is June, but I might have done something reckless," she admitted.

"Good, it's about time that you threw caution to the wind and had some fun. Let me guess, Mav finally convinced you to like him," Tilly said.

"You could say that," Melody mumbled. "And I told him that I like him."

"Well, that's fantastic," Tilly squealed.

"There's more," Melody said. "Um, we slept together."

"You what?" Tilly asked. "How did you two go from liking each other to jumping into bed together?"

"It's pretty easy to figure out," she mumbled. "I've had feelings for him since we met, and he said the same, and one thing led to another."

"And he got you naked and into his bed," Melody filled in the blanks.

"Yeah, do you hate me now?" she asked.

"How could I hate you? You're my sister and I'm happy for you as long as you're happy, Melody."

"Thanks, Tilly," she breathed. "I feel better that I told you before Owen did."

"Oh, well, you didn't exactly beat him to it. He texted me about an hour ago when you were still sleeping," Tilly admitted.

"And you let me go on and on while you knew the whole time?" Melody asked.

"I did. You know, I did like listening to you squirm a little bit. Besides, you are making a way bigger deal about this than was needed. You're a grown adult woman, and if you want to have sex with Mav, go for it," Tilly said. "And I am happy for you, Sis."

"Thanks," she said. "I'm pretty happy for me too, if I'm being honest. I'll call you soon."

"Please do," Tilly said, "my husband is good at sharing the news but awful at giving me details. I will expect full updates." Melody knew that it would be no good to refuse her sister. Tilly would just keep calling to bug her for information.

"Goodbye, Tilly," Melody said, smiling like a loon as she hung up the phone. Yeah, she was really happy for herself for the first time in a damn long time.

Melody joined the guys in the kitchen and Maverick handed her a plate of pancakes. "Saved you some breakfast," he said.

"Thanks," she whispered, sitting down at the table. June climbed up on the chair next to her and smiled. "Did you have a good breakfast, baby?" she asked.

"Yep," her toddler said, smiling over at her. "Mav made pancakes."

"You guys have been busy," Melody said, pouring some syrup over her pancakes. "Especially you, Owen."

"What does that mean?" he asked.

"My sister told me that you've been a busy bee texting her this morning," Melody said.

"Well, I thought she'd want to know about—" She wasn't about to let Owen finish that sentence. Melody held up her hand, effectively stopping him from saying that she slept with Maverick in front of everyone. It didn't matter that they all already knew—well, except her daughter who was too young to pick up on what was going on.

"I know what you texted her about, and I think it was my place to tell her about it, not yours," Melody chided.

"Noted, and for future reference, I'll keep that in mind," Owen promised. "How did she take the news?"

"She's fine with it," Melody said with a shrug. "I'd love to change the subject, please," she said, nodding to her daughter.

"Done," Maverick agreed. "How about we talk about the security measures that we're implementing?"

"Why do we need more security around here?" she asked.

"Because your husband was sneaking around our club looking for information about you and Maverick," Steel reminded.

"I'm aware, but I thought that Mav already had top-of-the-line security around here," she challenged.

"I do, but extra security won't hurt. We can't be too careful," Maverick insisted.

"So, we've got a few of the guys from the club stationed around the house," Owen said.

"That's very nice of them, but don't they have their own lives to get back to?" Melody asked. She hated to think that random strangers were giving up their personal time to keep an eye on her and her daughter. This was getting out of hand.

"Actually, they are patching into the club and it's part of their community service," Maverick said.

"Community service?" she asked. "Did they break the law?"

"No, when guys patch into the Road Reapers, Mace has them do things for him and other patched members of the club. You know—show their loyalty and prove their worth. It's kind of like when a fraternity hazes its potential members. We like to give the new guys a little shit before they become one of us," Owen said.

"Well, that sounds lovely," Melody teased. "I can see why guys want to join your club."

"Joke all you want to, but the Road Reapers are an exclusive MC and guys are lining up to get in," Owen said.

"Sorry," she mumbled. "I'm just grumpy this morning, I guess."

"Must be from lack of sleep," Maverick teased, giving her another outrageous wink, and making his brothers laugh.

"You are not helping," Melody said, pointing her finger at him for the full effect of her anger.

"What did I do?" he asked. She sighed, noticing that her daughter was taking in everything that they were saying.

"Can you watch June for a minute, Owen?" she asked. "I need to speak with Maverick privately." The guys all made a childish "Oohing" sound, and she rolled her eyes at them.

"Sure," Owen said. "Take your time yelling at my brother. June and I will be just fine. We'll find a cartoon to watch."

"I love cartoons," Steel said.

"Well, you can watch too. It will keep you and June quiet for a few minutes so that I can get started on the security upgrades," Owen said.

"Thanks, Owen," Melody said. "Let's go, Mav." She stood from her chair, crossed the kitchen, and grabbed his hand. Melody tugged him along with her to the master bedroom, careful not to let go of him for fear that he'd try to run back downstairs like a child.

"Is all of this really necessary?" he asked.

"Yes," she breathed, shutting the door behind them. "You can't tell your brothers our private information."

"Why not?" he asked.

"Are you kidding?" she growled. "I don't want the world to know that we're sleeping together."

"Why not?" he asked again.

"Because that's private information and I don't want everyone to know," she said. "What's happening between the two of us is just that—between the two of us."

"Okay, well, they are my brothers and the only two people in this world that I consider to be my friends. So, I shared some good news with my friends."

"Us having sex is good news?" she asked.

"Well, for me it was. Did you not have a good time, Melody?" he asked, crowding her personal space.

"You know that I had a good time," she said, taking a step back from him. Every step she took away from Mav, he took a giant one toward her. He wasn't going to let her run and when he backed her up against the wall, she knew that he had effectively trapped her.

"What are you doing?" she squeaked. "They are right downstairs."

"I know that, and that means that you're going to have to be quieter than you were last night, honey." He pulled her sweatpants and panties down her legs before she even knew what was happening. Maverick unbuttoned his jeans and let them fall to the floor with a thud. She was sure that his brothers would have a good idea about what they were doing up in the master bedroom, but for some odd reason, she didn't care. She wanted Maverick and having him take her with his brothers just downstairs did something to her girl parts that she wasn't expecting.

Maverick ran his fingers through her pussy and hummed his approval. "You like this, don't you?" he whispered into her ear. She wanted to moan but knew that it would only give away what they were doing. Instead, she bit her lip and nodded her agreement.

"You're such a naughty girl," he breathed as he kissed his way down her jawline to her lips. Maverick wasted no time thrusting into her wet pussy as he pulled her long legs around his waist. He set a punishing pace as he pumped in and out of her body, taking what he wanted from her and giving her so much more.

"I fucking love you, Melody," he growled. He stilled and she could tell that he wasn't sure if he had said what he just said out loud. "Shit, I'm sorry, honey," he whispered. "I didn't mean to say that out loud. I just got caught up in the moment."

She nodded and wrapped her arms around his neck. "I understand," she breathed. "When I'm with you, I tend to get caught up in the moment too, Mav." He leaned down to take her lips again, taking the out that she was giving him, but he had said the words that she had longed to hear from him over the past week of living in his house. Maybe it was too soon for grand, sweeping declarations, but she didn't care. Her heart belonged to Maverick and now, she knew that she owned his heart in return.

"I love you too, Mav," she breathed as she found her release. This time, he didn't stop taking what he needed from her. This time, he followed her over and pulled her limp body into his arms, carrying her off to the bathroom.

Maverick got them both naked, turning on the shower, and waiting for the water to heat. He pushed her into the warm spray and back up agist the shower wall. The way that he looked at her was nearly her undoing.

Maverick stroked her fading bruises and she winced. "Mine," he whispered. "You're mine, now, honey." She bit back the tears that threatened to fall from her eyes and nodded.

"I'm yours, Mav," she agreed. "Always."

MAVERICK

Having Melody and June in his space made life feel right to Maverick. He wanted to ask her to make it a permanent thing, but he had spent the last two months worrying that when the mess with her soon-to-be ex-husband was over, she'd leave him. They had talked about a future together, but he had no idea if she really meant it or not. Mav was used to people leaving him—first his parents, and then, his brothers when they both joined the military. What if Melody decided to leave him too? The one thing that he was sure of was that his heart wouldn't be able to stand losing her or June.

"What has you sitting alone in the kitchen, looking so pensive?" Melody asked. She walked into the room and wrapped her arms around his shoulders. He loved that she constantly seemed to need to touch him. He felt the same way about her.

"I was trying to figure a few things out, is all," he said. It wasn't the complete truth but giving her that might not end well for him.

"Has something happened that I need to know about? Is it Adam?" she asked.

"No," he breathed. "This has nothing to do with Adam. Honestly, I was sitting here thinking about us," he said, pulling her onto his lap.

"Us?" she asked. "What about us?"

"Well, I was wondering what will happen to us after this mess is all over. Say we can prove that Adam is now stalking you on top of the fact that he abused you and has threatened to take June from you—what happens when he's in prison?"

"I guess we'll figure that out when it happens, Mav. Right now, I can't think about the future until I get my present sorted out. You have to know that I meant it when I told you that I love you. I just can't make you any promises about what our future holds until Adam is in prison."

"I get that," he lied. His feelings were hurt that she could tell him that she loved him, yet not promise a future with him.

"I'm not trying to hurt you, Mav," she said. It was too late for that, but he wasn't going to be childish about it and throw a tantrum.

"So, if I asked you to marry me, what would you say?" he asked. The words were out before he could stop them. He wanted to kick himself, instead, he sat there holding his breath waiting for her to answer.

"I—I just can't do that right now, Mav," she said. "I appreciate the offer, but be realistic, I'm still married to Adam."

"Legally, sure," he said. Maverick hated that she was using her marriage to Adam as an excuse to not marry him. He'd wait for that asshole to be out of the picture, but she didn't even consider that option.

"Maverick, I just can't do this now. Can we please revisit this at another time? I'm tired and want to crawl into bed while June is sleeping," she said. He wanted to insist that they talk about their future now, but pushing things with Melody might ensure that he had no future with her, and that wasn't an option for him.

"Yeah, we can table my proposal for now, but just so you know that I wasn't just asking to ask—" Maverick reached into his pocket and pulled out a ring box that he had been carting around for almost two weeks now. Steel had gone into town with specific instructions from Mav on where to go and what kind of ring to pick up. His brother got it perfect too, and he was hoping that seeing the ring might help change her mind.

"You bought me a ring?" she asked. "When did you have time to get this?" she asked, reaching for the box. Her hands were shaking, and he could tell that she was on the verge of tears.

"I gave Steel all the information that he needed, and he went to town and picked it up for me," Maverick said. "Do you like it?" he hopefully asked.

"It's beautiful," she whispered, "I love it, but it doesn't change my answer. I can't give you one until I know what is going to happen with Adam." He pulled the ring box back from her reach and snapped it shut, shoving it into his pocket.

"Understood," he breathed. "You should get some sleep while you can."

"Mav," she said, reaching for his arm. He childishly pulled it free and sat back down at the kitchen table.

"We'll talk about it later," he said, giving her an out.

"I'm sorry," she whispered as she backed out of the room. The sobs that he heard from her as she made her way up to her room was nearly his undoing, but he refused to keep rehashing the conversation. Maverick let her go and that was something he worried that he might have to do again in the future—and that was going to break his heart.

Maverick felt like Melody had been sleeping forever. Sure, he was being dramatic, but he just couldn't help himself. She had shot him down and it hurt his damn feelings. Sulking and waiting for her to wake up was all he seemed capable of doing.

His cell phone ringing pulled him out of his self-imposed funk, and he grabbed it from the table and answered it.

"Yeah," he growled into the phone.

"Well, you sound grumpier than usual," Steel said. "Trouble in paradise?" There was no way that he'd admit to his brother that he had guessed correctly. The last thing he needed was for his brother to give him shit about Melody turning down his marriage proposal after he went and picked up the ring and everything.

"Shut the fuck up and tell me why you called me," Mav grumbled.

"Which is it?" Steel asked. "Do you want me to shut the fuck up or tell you why I called?"

"Stop being a smart ass and just tell me," Maverick ordered.

"Fine, Melody's husband was hanging around my apartment complex. The poor asshole thought that I was you. I told him to get lost or that I'd beat the shit out of him, and he had the nerve to just laugh at me. Can you believe that asshole?" Maverick could believe it. Adam was a pompous prick who didn't give a shit about threats.

"Yeah, that sounds like him," Maverick agreed. "Did you fill him in on the fact that you're my twin?"

"Nope," Steel admitted. "If he thinks I'm you, it might buy us some more time. Melody's court case is soon, right?"

"Yes, in a few weeks," Maverick said. He was both looking forward to it and dreading it all at the same time.

"Well, it doesn't matter to me who Adam thinks that I am. If he thinks that I have Melody and that I'm you, he'll keep coming back here and won't look any further," Steel said.

"But that puts you in danger," Maverick insisted.

"I know that you don't really believe this about me, but I can take care of myself. Uncle Sam has turned me into a killing machine, and I can use some of my acquired talents if need be." Maverick knew that his brother had some wicked newly acquired skills taught to him by the government, but he never imagined Steel being turned into a "Killing Machine" as he put it.

"We'll unpack that later," Maverick said. "Right now, I need you to promise me that you won't go and do anything stupid."

Steel barked out his laugh into the other end of the call. "I can make you no such promise, brother," he said. "What I can give you is time and space to get Melody to the courthouse for the hearing that will put this asshole away for a very long time." Maverick could tell that he wasn't going to change his brother's mind about this one. Once Steel stuck his heels in, there was no stopping him.

"I appreciate the assist, but if things go south, I want you to call me, got it?" Maverick asked.

"Got it," Steel agreed. "I'll let you know if he stops coming around her looking for you."

"That would be great," Maverick agreed. "Just don't take any unnecessary risks, Steel."

"Again, no promises," Steel repeated. "Have a good night and talk soon." His brother ended the call and Steel tossed his cell phone back to the kitchen table. He had a feeling that things were about to go sideways. He usually did well with his gut feelings and right now, his gut was screaming at him that nothing was going to work out the way that he wanted it too.

MELODY

Melody woke up to Maverick shouting June's name and she panicked. The last thing she remembered was Mav showing her an engagement ring and her turning him down flat—for now.

"June, come on out, honey," Maverick shouted.

Melody pulled on her robe and walked out into the hallway to find him pacing from room to room. "What's going on?" she asked. "Where is June?"

"I came up to check on you both and she wasn't in her bed. I must have fallen asleep on the sofa after Steel called me and when I woke up, she was gone."

"She can't be gone," Melody insisted. "She's two. Where would she go by herself? I don't think that she can even open your front door. Did you check the cameras?" she asked.

"No, I panicked and didn't take the time to. I thought that she just might be hiding," Maverick admitted.

"You check the cameras and I'll search for her," Melody

ordered. She was usually good in a pinch, keeping her cool when others panicked. Melody searched under beds, in closets, and even in the bathtub for her daughter and when Maverick came back upstairs with a disturbed look on his face, she wanted to be sick.

"What's happened?" she breathed. "Did you find something?"

"I did," he said, "Adam was here. He somehow got into the house through one of the downstairs windows, after he disabled my security system. Your husband is quite crafty. He grabbed her while she was sleeping. That's why we didn't hear them. June was asleep the whole time he was carrying her out of here. I'm so sorry that I allowed this to happen," Maverick said.

"Oh God, he's got her," Melody whispered. "He said that he'd get to her, and he did."

"We need to call the police," Maverick said. "We need to report this so that they can find her."

Melody pulled her cell phone from the pocket of her robe and tried Adam's number. His smug voice over the line was nearly her undoing. "I take it you figured it all out then," he said. "I knew that you would. You were always a smart woman."

"I want my daughter back, Adam," Melody breathed. Losing her temper with him usually ended badly for her and now, he'd take out his anger on June and she couldn't allow that.

"She's my daughter too, Melody," he said. "But you seem to have forgotten about our family since you hooked up with that biker." He was grasping at straws, and she wasn't about to play his game.

"Don't do this to June," Melody begged. "She needs me."

"She needs her father too, Melody," Adam challenged. "How about you meet me, and we can talk about the three of us being a family again?" he asked. Adam knew that using her daughter to get her to do what he wanted was a plan that might just work. It was how he kept her tethered to his side for so long.

"Where are you?" she whispered. Maverick groaned and shook his head at her. There was no way that he'd let her go, but then again, she wasn't planning on giving him a choice in the matter.

"You know where you can find me," he said.

"No, I don't, Adam," she shouted into the phone. "Tell me where you are, and I'll come to you."

"You'll figure it out, I'm sure," Adam said, ending the call.

"Shit," she shouted, throwing her phone across the room.

"You are not serious about going to meet with him," Maverick insisted.

"I'll do whatever it takes to get my daughter back," she spat. "But that asshole didn't tell me where to find them."

"Thank God for small favors," Maverick breathed. "Let's try this my way. I think that we need to involve the police." Melody nodded, seeing no other choice in the matter.

"Call them," she agreed. She sunk to her daughter's bed, pulling her favorite stuffed bunny into her arms, and hugging it close. She wasn't sure how, but she planned on getting her little girl back, no matter what it might cost her.

"The police are here," Maverick said, ducking his head into June's room. Melody refused to leave her daughter's bed, still wearing her bathrobe. She didn't care what anyone else thought, getting to her daughter was her only priority, even if it might cost Melody her freedom or even her life.

"I'll be right down," she mumbled.

"We're going to find her," Maverick promised.

"I don't want promises that you can't keep, Mav," she spat. God, she sounded like a first-class bitch, but she just couldn't seem to help but lash out at him. "Your security system was supposed to keep both of us safe," she reminded.

"You're right," he agreed, "and, I feel awful as it is. Let's focus on finding June and then, you can ream me out for my short callings after she is safe back here with us." He was right. She needed to focus on how to find Adam and then, she'd get her daughter back.

By the time she got downstairs to the kitchen, the police had already asked Maverick questions about his security system and were looking at the footage showing Adam taking June from the house while she and Maverick were napping. How could she let her guard down? That wasn't something that she planned on doing again.

"Can you find my daughter?" she asked, interrupting the police officer from asking Maverick yet another question about his security camera.

"We're going to try, Ma'am," the officer said. "Can you tell us about your ex-husband? Is there a custody agreement in place?"

"No, and he's still my husband. I left him after he abused me again. There should be an arrest record on file for the night that I finally filed charges against him. Our court date is coming up in a few weeks and hopefully, my divorce will be approved around that same time, but we have no formal custody agreement. I do have a restraining order against him."

"Well, that's helpful," the officer said. "He violated the agreement when he showed up to this house. That alone will land him back in jail and he'll probably be denied bail this time."

"That's some good news," Maverick said. Nothing sounded

like good news to her right now. She wanted June back, and then, she planned on making sure that Adam spent the rest of his life behind bars so that he'd never be able to touch either of them again.

"Do you have any idea where your husband might be?" the officer asked. She thought back to their phone conversation and had gone over Adam's clues in her head while she was waiting for the police to show up. Melody had a pretty good idea where her husband was holding their daughter, but there was no way that she was going to share that information with the cops. No, she was going to do what Adam instructed her to do and show up alone to talk about the three of them. He wasn't going to like what she had to say about them being a family again, but he'd get over it soon enough.

"No clue," she lied. She was betting that Adam would take June back to their house—the one she swore that she'd never go back to. The one thing that life was teaching her was to never say never.

"If you come up with anything or he calls you, please be in touch," the officer said, handing her his card.

"Will do, thank you for coming out," she said. She waited for Maverick to show the officer out before heading up to take a shower. She gave him some excuse about needing some alone time and she wasn't sure if he suspected that she was up to something or if he was just hurt by the way that she was pushing him away. It didn't matter right now though. Melody knew what she was going to have to do and involving Maverick would only end up getting him killed. Going home to her abusive husband, to save her little girl, was something that she was going to have to do on her own. It was the only way.

MAVERICK

Maverick knew that finding Melody at her old place was a long shot. The house had been empty since he had moved both her and June in with him, but he had a sinking feeling that her ex would try to lure her back to their former home. It was poetic, really, even if the thought of her ex touching her in any way made him sick.

What really pissed him off was the way that Melody snuck off in the night, disappearing the way that June had earlier, but this time, he was awake for the whole thing. Melody had no idea that he was watching her dress in the dark bedroom before she grabbed her purse and snuck out of the house. He had Steel waiting for her outside, but she didn't know that either. It was all a part of his plan to make sure that he or one of his brothers had eyes on her at all times. It was the only way to make sure that she didn't go off and get herself killed during her crazy plan to get June back on her own. It killed him that she didn't seem to trust him enough to include him in her plan, but then again, he did fail at keeping her daughter safe in the first place.

Steel followed her back to her old house, proving Maverick's theory correct. Adam was holding June there and Melody had figured it out too. According to Steel's text, she walked into the house like she was returning home after a trip to the grocery store—as if the last few months hadn't happened. As if she hadn't ever agreed to belong to Maverick. He was going to have to put his butt-hurt feelings aside for the time being if he wanted to get her and June out of there alive. And with his brother's help, that's exactly what he planned on doing.

Maverick pulled into the back alley behind the house and cut his lights and engine. He didn't want to attract any unwanted attention. Steel knocked on his passenger side window and he unlocked his truck, letting his brother into his vehicle.

"She's in there," Steel said, nodding to the house. "Just walked right in and hasn't come out since I texted you. It's been pretty quiet too."

"Shit, I've got to get in there," Maverick growled.

"You can't just go rushing into that house. You'll get yourself and Melody killed. He wants the kid because she'll get him Melody. He won't hurt June," Steel guessed.

"No, but he'll hurt Melody. We both know what he's capable of doing to her," Maverick breathed. He remembered walking in through the kitchen door months ago and finding Adam beating the shit out of Melody. He wanted to rip the guy apart for laying one finger on her, but Melody took care of her husband all on her own.

"Right, and we both know what Melody is capable of doing to her ex if he lays a finger on her. Your girl is quite capable of taking care of herself," Steel said. "Owen has eyes on the front of the house and Mace is with him. We've called the cops, and they should be here any minute. We'll get her out of there and you'll be alive tomorrow to talk about it," Steel said.

"I'm not sure that she's still my girl," Maverick mumbled more to himself.

"What do you mean?" Steel asked. "You fuck things up somehow?"

"Yep," Maverick admitted. "I fell asleep when I should have been watching the house. I allowed her husband an opportunity to get to June and I'm betting that Melody will never forgive me." He was sure that he had lost her and there would be no getting her back, even if they were lucky enough to get her out of that house alive.

"That's bullshit, Mav," Steel insisted. "You and I both know it. Mace had two guys watching the house and they missed Adam slipping past your security too. He got past everyone, not just you. Plus, you can't stay awake forever. It happened," Steel said. "Adam got to June, and now, you're going to get both her and Melody back. Just don't fuck things up with her when you get a second chance. She's a good woman and I'm not sure why she seems to want you, but she does. Just remember that when this mess is all over."

"Thanks, man," Maverick said. "I'm not sure that I quite believe most of what you just said, but one thing is for sure—I don't deserve her, but I'm going to work my ass off to win her back."

"That's the spirit," Steel said. "Now, how about you and I get our asses up to the back of the house to keep an eye on things until the cops get here. If things go sideways, we'll head in, but I'll need you to agree to follow my lead."

"Don't I always?" Maverick grumbled.

"No," Steel said. "You don't, but I'm hoping that things have changed since I've been away. You were always the stubborn brother."

"Shut the fuck up and let's go," Maverick said. Steel waited for Maverick to flank his side before making his way to the back of the house, his gun in hand.

"How come you get one of those and I don't?" Maverick asked.

"Because mine is government-issued and you don't have a permit to carry," Steel reminded. Maverick had gotten himself into a little bit of trouble as a teenager and getting a gun permit wasn't something that was high on his priority list.

"Good point," Maverick breathed. They made their way up to the back of the house and he peeked through the window to find Melody standing in the corner of the room as Adam paced in front of her. There was no sign of June in the room, and he hoped that she was safe in another part of the house.

"He's got a gun," Steel said.

"Yeah, I see that," Maverick whispered back. "I can't just leave her in there."

"Yes, you can," Steel said. "I do this kind of thing for a living and I'm damn good at it. Let me do my job, Mav," he whispered. Adam shouted something at Melody, and she cried out for him to stop. Maverick knew that he could make Adam stop doing or saying whatever he was saying if he could just get into that house.

"No, I can't," Maverick breathed. He ran for the back door with Steel hot on his heels.

"Move," Steel shouted, pushing Maverick out of the way. He was the first one into the kitchen and got a shot off before

Maverick made it in through the back door. Steel hit Adam's right shoulder, and he dropped the gun from his hand.

"Shit," Adam shouted. He bent to grab the gun with his left hand, but before he got the chance, Melody grabbed a frying pan from the stove and hit him in the back of the head, just as she had done months before when Maverick found her in this same kitchen.

"See," Steel said, looking back at him, "your girl is ruthless." Adam slumped onto the floor and Melody dropped the frying pan with a thud beside him.

"Is he dead?" she asked.

"I don't think so," Steel admitted. "We're just not that lucky. But he's going to prison and this time, he won't make bail."

"Thank God," Melody breathed.

Maverick wanted to cross the kitchen and pull Melody into his arms, but he wasn't sure if that was a good idea or not. "You okay, honey?" he asked.

"I'm not sure what I am," she admitted.

"Where's June?" Steel asked.

"She's upstairs in her bedroom. Hopefully, she slept through this whole ordeal," Melody said. "Shouldn't we call the cops?" she asked.

"They are already here," Owen said, walking in through the front of the house. Mace was by his side and two police officers followed them into the kitchen. "You okay?" Owen asked, pulling Melody in for a quick hug.

"I will be," she breathed.

"He's been shot," Maverick said to the officers. "He'll need an ambulance."

"I also hit him with a frying pan," Melody whispered. "Again."

"I'll call for an ambulance while you take statements." One of the officers disappeared into the family room to call for an ambulance and the second officer asked Melody what happened. She sat down at the kitchen table and told the officer how she snuck out of Maverick's house and figured out where to find Adam. He told her that he wanted her back and when she refused his offer, he pulled out a gun and threatened to kill her. That was the point where Steel and Maverick barged into the kitchen and stopped Adam from making good on his threats.

Hearing the whole story made him sick. He hated that he didn't stop her from sneaking out, but then again, Maverick knew that once Melody set her mind to something, she wouldn't let anyone stop her.

The police finally finished up questioning them all and Melody looked about ready to collapse. "Can you take June and me home, Mav?" she asked. He liked the fact that she still thought of his place as home. He at least had that going for him.

"Of course," he agreed.

"The cops said that if they have any more questions for you, they'll be in touch. Adam is being taken into surgery now, but they will keep him under guard at the hospital as he recovers," Owen said. "He's going to prison and won't be getting out anytime soon."

"I'll finally be free of him and will be able to get a divorce," Melody breathed. Maverick didn't want to get his hopes up that her being rid of Adam might mean that she'd actually want a life with him. He had made her the offer once and she had already turned him down.

"Looks that way," Owen agreed. "Are you sure that you're okay? Would you like to come back to stay with Tilly and me?" Owen asked. Maverick wanted to protest until Steel put his hand on his shoulder, silently stopping him.

"I'm sure," Melody said. "I'd really like to get June back to Maverick's place. She's familiar with her surroundings there and will be comfortable. I'm worried that she might remember some parts of today and I want her to be in a familiar setting."

"Then, let's get you both home," Maverick said.

"I'll grab June," Steel offered.

Maverick helped Melody with her jacket and grabbed her purse. "Is there anything else you want from here?" he asked.

Melody looked around the room and shook her head. "No," she whispered, "I don't want anything from this place—not even my memories, but I can't get rid of those." He couldn't blame her for wanting to leave everything in the past because that's where he wanted to leave this entire mess. The only good thing to come out of this was Melody moving into his house and his bed.

They drove in silence and Maverick was grateful for it. He needed to get his head straight before they got back to his place. Hell, he needed to get his heart straight before Melody tore it out of his chest and handed it to him. He was sure that was how things were going to play out.

He carried June up to her room and put her into her bed, kissing her little forehead. The kid had slept through the whole adventure, but they wouldn't be sure until she woke up. Hopefully, she wouldn't remember a thing about her father taking her from his house and holding her mother at gunpoint.

Maverick found Melody sitting on his bed and joined her, sitting on the edge next to her. "You okay?" he asked.

"Everyone keeps asking me that, and I'm not sure how to answer," she admitted. "I mean, I am okay, but I'm not—does that make sense?" she asked.

"It does," he agreed. "When my mom died, I felt that same way. I was okay, but I wasn't. It took a long time for me to be okay again and I have a feeling that the same was true for both of my brothers too. Take all the time that you need to feel okay again, honey," he said. "I'm not going anywhere."

"Really?" she asked. "You're not mad that I snuck off?"

"Oh, I'm good and pissed that you snuck off and didn't tell me, but that's something that we'll work through. You have to be angry with me that Adam got to June and took her." He felt as though he was holding his breath waiting for her to give her answer.

"I was, at first, but then I realized that he would have gotten in here anyway. He wanted June and taking her was always his plan to hurt me. There was nothing that you could have done to stop him and if you had tried, he probably would have killed you. We're all here, and we are all safe. For now, that's enough," Melody said.

"Thank you for that, honey," he said. "And for the record, I knew the whole time that you were planning on sneaking out. I even watched you get changed in the dark. My brothers were waiting outside to follow you until I could get dressed and come after you."

"You knew what I was planning?" she asked.

"I did," he admitted, "I guess I know you a little bit better than you thought I did," he said.

"Yeah, I guess you do," she agreed. "So, what are we going to do now?"

"Now, I'm going to give you the time and space that you

need," he offered. He didn't want to do it, but if it was what Melody needed, he would. "I'm going to take the spare room and you can have our bed."

"No," she almost shouted. She reached for him, and he took her hand into his own. "I don't need you to give me time or space," she whispered. "When I was standing in my old kitchen, watching Adam swing his gun around at me, I knew that I had made an awful mistake."

"By sneaking off?" he asked.

"No, by telling you that I needed more time to consider your marriage proposal. I freaked out when you pulled out that beautiful ring that you bought for me. I wasn't sure what my future was going to be as long as Adam was looking for me and June. But you were so patient with me and gave me the time that I needed. I don't need any more time though. I know what my answer is going to be."

"You do?" he asked. He wasn't sure if he wanted to ask her what it was going to be, but he also needed to know. The hope that welled up in his chest had him nearly panting. "And," he prompted.

"And, I'd love to be your wife, Maverick," she whispered. "As long as you're good with waiting for me to get rid of my abusive asshole of a husband, I'm ready to agree to marry you."

"I'll wait as long as it takes for you to be my wife, honey," he said. Maverick meant it too. He'd wait forever for Melody to officially be his. He never saw himself settled down with an instant family, yet here he was. Melody was his girl, and now, she'd soon be his wife. She was the woman he wanted riding shotgun with him for the rest of his life, and she was finally agreeing to do just that.

Six Months Later

Maverick knew that his brother wanted to see him to try to convince him to take on more responsibility at the security firm. He just didn't want to sign on for a full-time position because he didn't want to give up his bike shop. But Owen said that he had a compromise that might work for both of them. He just never imagined that it would involve his twin brother, Steel.

They both showed up at his bike shop and Mav was beginning to feel like he was being ganged up on. He groaned, "When you both show up at the same time, I feel like I'm not going to like what's about to happen. Tell me I'm wrong this time, and that you both aren't going to gang up on me," he insisted.

"Can't do that," Steel admitted. "But I think that you might actually like what we're about to gang up on you about."

"I've found the perfect place for my security business," Owen said.

"That's great," Maverick said. "I was getting sick of running across town every time you needed me to come in. Wait—is it still across town?"

"Nope, it's a bit closer," Owen said. Steel laughed and Maverick wondered what the two of them were up to.

"You know that building next door?" The old tenant had moved out of the building next door that Maverick owned. He had bought both buildings when he decided to go into business for himself and rented out the one across the alley. Maverick was worried that he'd never find someone to rent that building out to. It had been six months since his old tenant had moved out and he was beginning to give up hope.

"You want to rent my building?" he asked.

"Nope," Owen said, "I want to buy your building. I know that having it sit empty stresses you out, and I want to take some of the stress off your shoulders."

"Can you afford it?" Maverick asked. "I mean, I won't charge you what I'd charge others, but can you still swing it?"

"He can because I've agreed to be a partner in the firm," Steel said. Maverick was hoping that his brother was planning on sticking around for a while. Steel wasn't the type of guy to stay in one place for very long. It's why the military was such a good choice for him. But now that he was out of the military, Maverick secretly hoped that his brother would hang around and maybe even put down roots.

"So, you're sticking around?" Mav asked.

"Yep, and I'm joining the firm—on one condition," Steel said. He was almost scared to ask what the one condition might be, but he had to know.

"One condition?" Maverick asked.

"Yep—I want you to become the third partner in the firm. If the three of us work together, you should be able to keep this place on the side, especially since the new building is literally right across the alley." Steele made a good point, but how could he commit to giving his brothers his full attention and keeping his bike shop?

"You can hire someone to help around here for times that you're on the job for the firm. I'm sure that you'll be able to find someone from down at the club who is good at fixing bikes," Owen said. He could think of a few guys who had helped him out in a jam over the years when he was slammed with too many bikes to fix and not enough hours in a day.

"I know of a few guys," he said, "but, is the three of us

working together full-time a good idea?" he asked. He and his brothers seemed to find a way to fight like crazy when they spent too much time together. He believed that it was one of the reasons why Steel had spent so much time away from home—to get away from him and Owen.

"We'll find a way to make it work," Steel assured. "Besides, we're grown-ass men now. We might not always see eye to eye, but we can agree to disagree without starting a fight."

"I agree with Steel," Owen said. They both looked so hopeful, that he couldn't tell them that he didn't want to be a part of the security firm that Owen was building, and now, with the new conditions, he didn't want to.

"Why not talk to Melody about this and get back to us," Steel said.

"I don't need to talk to Melody about this," Maverick said. "I already know what she's going to say. She'll tell me to do it and I have to admit, I would agree with her. Besides, we could use the extra money now that we'll have an extra mouth to feed."

"An extra mouth?" Steel asked.

"Yep, you two are going to be uncles again," Maverick said. He knew that his brothers already considered June to be their niece. Hell, they spoiled her rotten, but now, they were going to have another baby to spoil.

"Melody is pregnant?" Owen asked.

"She is," Maverick said, "we just found out last week that she's about four months along now."

"Wow, congratulations, man," Steel said, slapping his brother on the back.

"Yeah, I kind of already knew, since Melody told her sister. Those two can't keep a secret to save their lives. Tilly is excited to be an aunt again," he said. "Congrats, Mav,"

"Thanks guys," he said. "So, we're going to do this then?" he asked.

"I'm in," Steel said.

"It was my idea, so I'm in," Owen agreed.

"Well, then, I'm in too," Maverick added. He wasn't sure how this was going to work out—the three of them in business together, but he kind of liked the idea of it. He was happy to have both of his brothers close again, and with any luck, this new business venture would keep them around for a very long time.

The End

I hope you enjoyed Maverick and Melody's story. Don't miss book three of the Dirty Riders MC Series, coming soon. Here's a sneak peek at Riding Steel!

STEEL

Steel Blaine watched as Justice paced in front of his makeshift desk. He really needed to go shopping for office furniture, but who had the time? Since joining his two brothers in their security team, he didn't have one second to himself. His folding table worked just fine as a desk, and it also allowed him to believe that he'd be able to pick up and move on if necessary. A big, heavy desk would void that possibility and that wasn't something he was willing to think about right now. No, right now, he had to decide what to do about the sexy blond nervously pacing in front of him.

"I know it sounds crazy, Steel, but I can feel him out there watching me. I've already been to two cities for my book tour, and he showed up at both of them," Justice said.

"Wait, you've seen this guy?" Steel asked.

"I have and he's not shy about letting me know that he's around." Justice pulled her phone out of her purse and handed it over to him. "Those are all texts from him." He read through the disgusting texts and grimaced at the ones that were explicit requests that made him want to take the job for her on the spot.

"He has your number?" Steel asked, already knowing the answer to his question. He was holding the proof that the guy had her phone number.

"Yeah. I'm not sure how he got it, but he's been texting me for months now," she admitted.

"Jesus, Justice," he growled. "Why didn't you come to me sooner, or at least change your fucking number?" he asked.

"Because we didn't leave things on the best terms," she reminded. Justice was right. The last time he saw her, he acted like an asshole. The last thing she probably wanted to do was reach out to him and ask him for his help.

"Plus, I've been kind of busy with my writing, and I guess that I was just hoping that this mess would go away on its own," she admitted. He knew just how busy she had been with her writing. Justice had built quite a name for herself over the past year, even landing a seven-book series deal with a big publisher. He had followed every step of her impressive career, but there was no way that he'd admit that to her. She already had one stalker; he didn't want her to think that he was stalking her too.

"Obviously, this guy isn't going to go away if he's still sending you these messages and following you around on your book tour," Steel said.

Justice rolled her eyes at him, "Obviously," she grumbled. "Listen, maybe coming to you for help was a mistake. I should have realized that you'd still be pissed off at me. I just never imagined that you'd be holding a grudge or anything as childish as all that." She took her phone back from him and put it into her purse. "Tell Owen and Mav that I said, 'Hey'," she said, turning to leave.

"Justice, wait," he growled. The words were out of his mouth before he could even think them over. She was right—he was acting like a child and that wasn't how he wanted things to play out between him and Justice. "I was an idiot back in high school," he admitted. He was too. Justice was the prettiest girl in the whole school, and she liked him. His problem was that she told him that she liked him, and his stupid mouth got in the way of him giving her the words back. In fact, Steel had made up some stupid lie about not liking her and liking her best friend, Julie, instead. He took things too far by asking Julie out to prom and that was about the time that Justice had quit talking to him. He graduated, watched his mom die from cancer, joined the Navy, and he didn't look back. Steel stayed away from home for as long as possible, letting his twin brother, Maverick, and his little brother, Owen, handle everything on the home front. He wasn't the kind of guy looking to put down roots and Justice was the kind of girl who would have required that commitment from him.

"Wait for what, Steel?" she asked. "Wait for you to break my heart again? Wait for you to take off again when things get too hard to handle? What am I waiting for now?" she asked. He deserved that from her. She had every right to question him and the reasons why he was asking her to wait.

"I'm sorry about all of that, Justice," he insisted. "I should have never asked Julie out. I lied about even liking her and took things too far." He had admitted all of that to Julie at prom, ruining their whole night together, but he just couldn't help himself. Self-sabotage was his go-to move, and he was pretty damn good at it.

"Yeah, Julie told me all about what you said to her and how you hurt her. How could you do that to her at prom?" she asked.

"Because I'm an ass," he said. "But you already knew that. I'm sorry for all of it," he said. "I should have been honest with you from the beginning, but I wasn't."

"Yeah, and what would that have looked like, Steel?" she asked. "You know—you being honest with me."

"It would have looked like me telling you that I liked you too, but I was too afraid to say those words out loud. My mom was sick, and we didn't know how sick until Mav, and I graduated. Watching her fade away was a lot for teenage boys to handle. I guess I was afraid that if it told you how I felt about you, you'd disappear too, just like she did. It's why I've been away from home for so long now." The only reason he had come home was to be closer to his brothers. It didn't hurt that Justice was still in town and still single, but he wasn't holding out hope that she'd ever forgive him for how he treated her back in high school.

"I'm sorry that you had to go through all of that, Steel. I wish you would have let me in to help you, but that's not what I need right now," she said. "I'm not standing here telling you that I like you," she said. "I'm asking you to let me hire you. I need someone to go with me on the rest of my book tours this year, and I was hoping that you'd want the job. I don't trust a lot of people, but I trust you, for what it's worth." Hearing her say that was worth more than she'd ever know. There was no way that he'd let her down again.

"I'll take the job," he quickly agreed.

"Wait—what?" she asked.

"I'll take the job," he repeated.

"You will?" she asked again.

"Yep," he said.

"It's going to be a lot of travel," she said.

"I'm okay with travel, as long as you're good with paying my travel expenses," he teased.

"Um, yes," she said. "I will pay for everything. Thank you, Steel," she said. Justice held out her hand to him and he walked around his makeshift desk to shake it.

"You are welcome," he said.

"Oh—just one other thing," she quickly added. "I don't want anyone knowing about my stalker—especially not my publisher."

"Okay, can I ask why?" he asked.

"Because the guy who's stalking me used to work for my publisher and I don't want to lose my contract with them. Can you make me that one promise?" she asked. "They can never know." Well, that solved the mystery of how he got her number and how he seemed to know where she was going to be and when. All Steel had to do now was figure out why this asshole was going after Justice and then, he'd be able to keep her safe.

"Deal," he agreed. "No one will know about your stalker."

"Or that you're my bodyguard," she said. "If my publisher finds out that you're my bodyguard, she'll start asking questions that I don't want to answer."

"What are we going to tell them?" he asked. "I mean, if I'm traveling from town to town with you, won't your publisher become suspicious?" he asked.

"Well, I've thought about that and maybe we could tell her that you're my boyfriend," she squeaked out the word boyfriend and her cheeks turned the cutest shade of pink. Yeah, taking this assignment was going to be a whole lot more fun than he originally thought, and watching Justice squirm was going to be the best part.

JUSTICE

Justice Hanks wasn't sure how she was going to convince Steel to pretend to be her boyfriend, but she really had no other options. Sure, she had left out the part about her stalker not only working for her publisher but also being married to the head of the company.

She reported directly to Janine McDermont and her husband was the biggest slimeball in the industry. Everyone knew it—well, except Justice, but she quickly picked up on that fact when the guy stuck his hand down her skirt and said some of the dirtiest things she had ever heard. Devin McDermott was the foulest human she had ever met, and that was saying a lot. Janine had booked her a six-month book tour with a European extension if all went well with the US portion. She was finally living her dream but Devin showing up at her signings wasn't part of the plan.

At first, she thought that Janine had sent him to check up on her at her first signing, but she quickly found out that wasn't the truth when Janine told her that Devin had quit the firm. He had accepted an offer at another publishing house and Janine was livid. She said that she couldn't believe that her husband would betray her that way, and Justice knew that telling her about Devin's other betrayals wouldn't end well for her. How could she kick a woman while she was down? The truth was, she couldn't. The longer she let things go, and the more Devin showed up at her signings, the more she knew that she was in trouble.

He started sending her those disgusting text messages and that's when she started to really worry. The last few were raunchy and suggested that he was going to show up at her home. That was her last safe haven and Justice knew what she had to do. She had to go to Steel, of all people, and ask him for help.

"Wait—you want me to pretend to be your boyfriend?" Steel asked.

"I do," she agreed. "I need my publicist to think that everything is going smoothly so that my book tour doesn't get canceled."

"Does she have any idea?" he asked.

"I don't think so," Justice said. "Will you do it?" she asked. "Will you take the job and pretend to be my boyfriend?"

He let out his breath and dropped her hand from his own. She thought for sure that he was going to turn her down. "I'll do it," he said, surprising her. "But you need to talk to your publicist. If this guy keeps showing up, it's going to become a problem." He had no idea just how right he was, but the less he knew about her situation, the better. All Steel needed to know was that she had a stalker and he needed to keep her stalker away from her. Justice would have to find a way to handle the rest of it when the time came.

"I'll take care of everything else," she agreed. "Now, I need to get home and hang up a few of the security cameras that I just picked up."

Steel groaned and sat back down behind the crappy folding table that he was using as a desk. His office looked as though it was thrown together with things that he found in his basement. "I'm assuming that he knows where you live?" he asked.

"He does and he's told me that he plans on stopping by. I can't let that happen. My home is my place of refuge. I write there and if he shows up, unwanted, I don't know what I'll do."

"You'll move in with your new boyfriend who already has a great security system in place," Steel drawled.

"I think that you're overestimating my new boyfriend's enthusiasm about our relationship," she teased. Steel threw back his head and laughed and Justice was suddenly transported back to high school, staring at him as though he was the most beautiful boy in the whole world.

"I think that your new boyfriend would be fine with you moving into his place for a while," Steel said.

"Is your place decorated like your office?" she asked, looking around the messy room.

"What's that supposed to mean?" he asked.

"It means, you really don't have much in the way of furniture and my place is cozy. I even have a home office set up as my writing space. If I move into your place, I won't get much writing done and I'm on a deadline," she said. Her publisher had her on a tight deadline and not meeting it wasn't an option.

"Okay, how about if your new boyfriend sets up a real security system at your house and then moves in with you for a while, just to make sure that this creep doesn't show up there?" he asked. She had to think about that one. On one hand, having

Steel around would give her a sense of security, but on the other hand, he'd be a giant distraction and one that if she wasn't careful could cost Justice her heart again.

"I don't know if that's a good idea," she insisted.

"Listen, you want to hire me to keep you safe. If your stalker knows where you live, I'll need to put in better security measures than just sticking up a few store-bought cameras. At least let me put in a good security system for you, Justice. We can negotiate the rest later." Steel was right—she was hiring him to keep her safe and that meant while she was at home too.

"Fine," she said, "you can come over and put in a security system."

"Great, I'll grab something for us to eat and be over by five," he said. "I just have one client to check in on and then, I'll grab my gear."

"Something to eat?" she asked. "You don't have to get us food, Steel."

"Sure I do," he said. "It's the least I can do to make up for being an ass to you in high school."

"I hate to tell you this, but it's going to take more than one dinner to make up for all of that," she said.

"Noted," Steel said, "and, if you let me move in to keep an eye on you, it will give me more opportunities to make things up to you and clear my good name." Justice couldn't help her giggle as she shook her head at him. One thing she knew about Steel was that he was a smooth talker when he wanted to be. She had noticed him charming his way around town over the past few months that he had been home and joined his brothers' security team. The women all over town were vying to get his eye, but Steel seemed blind to all their efforts.

"I'll consider it," she lied. There was no way that she'd let

Steel move into her home to sweet talk her like he did the general female population in town. No, she had learned her lesson when it came to falling for Steel Blane—the hard way. The one thing she knew about herself after all these years was that she was a quick learner, and second chances were the only way to let people in to hurt her. Justice wouldn't be making that mistake again.

Riding Steel (Dirty Riders MC Series Book 3) universal link-> https://books2read.com/u/mdqy9w

What's releasing next from K.L.? Here's a sneak peek! Be the first to get your hands on The Lone Star Rangers Six Book Box Set coming February 2024!

ANDERS

Anders Justin Taylor III—yeah, it sounded like he should be someone he wasn't. With a name like that, he should have been born to a rich family—maybe tied to oil or cattle, especially in Texas. But he wasn't. Hell, he wasn't tied to much of anything in the small, shit town he grew up in. He was what the neighborhood kids liked to call whiskey tango—code for white trash. When he used to pass by those assholes in the hallways of the shithole high school that they all attended, he'd hear their whispers. As if calling him whiskey tango would sting any less. He got into a lot of fights over that nickname until he met his best friend—Whiskey O'Brian. Those high school fuckers weren't sure what to make of a kid actually named Whiskey and when the two of them faced down the bullies who dared called them names, no one was left standing to whisper at them as they walked down the hallways.

His dad had left him and his mom when he was about three. At least, that's what his Ma told him. He didn't remember the fucker and why should he? He was an alcoholic and an abusive husband to boot. That asshole walking away was the best thing that ever happened to him and his Ma, not that she'd admit it. He knew that a part of her still wondered where her husband disappeared to. Anders wondered if the asshole showed back up to their shit town if his mother would take him back—probably but that wasn't his problem anymore. He got out and there was no way he'd be sucked back into that place.

He grew up and got a scholarship to Georgetown and graduated at the top of his class with a degree in Criminal Justice. He thought he wanted to be a lawyer but when the FBI came calling, he jumped at his chance to join them. He worked his way up the ladder in a short time and became one of their most decorated agents specializing in bringing down drug cartels. That's how he hooked his best friend, Whiskey, into joining his team.

Whiskey had made a few wrong turns in life after he got out of the Air Force and he ended up working for the wrong guys. Hell, Miguel Diaz was at the top of the list of wrong guys to work for. He was considered the "God Father" of the drug world in Mexico and bringing that asshole down was the biggest boost to Anders's career to date. He wasn't quite sure how he had gotten so lucky to land a big fish like Diaz, but he had him. Diaz was six feet under—dead in the ground and Anders regretted nothing. The rest of Diaz's guys were in federal prison for running drugs over the Mexican border into the US and most of them were doing time on several murder charges. Yeah—those fuckers weren't going anywhere. Now, he had his sights set on bringing down the whole Guadalajara syndicate and that wasn't going to be easy by any stretch of the word.

He also had his work cut out for him tracking down a lead that Marcos Diego was still alive. Anders thought his friend had given his life trying to keep Luciana Diaz alive and safe on her way to Whiskey, but his source told him that Marc was alive and being held by the same syndicate he was trying to cut down. He and Whiskey were supposed to leave in the morning and head back down to Mexico, running down leads to Marcos' position. This would be their third trip down trying to track him and every time they got close, the Camillos would move him, and they'd come home empty-handed. He was starting to see the toll that it was taking on Whiskey's wife, Luciana since she felt guilty that Marcos was in this situation because of her, but it wasn't her fault that her father was a drug lord. Anders knew that Whiskey wouldn't rest until they brought Marc home, to give his wife some peace of mind, and he had to agree—he wouldn't stop until Marcos was back in the States, safe and sound.

First, he was going to tackle dating even though he knew it was a fucking bad idea. He let Whiskey and Luci set him up on a blind date. Hell, he didn't even go on regular dates, and this was a fucking awful idea, but he needed to get laid and Whiskey was right—he wasn't getting any younger. He had moved back to Texas, following Whiskey and his new little family to a small town just outside of Huston. Anders loved that he was close enough to all four major FBI field offices in Houston, El Paso, Dallas, and San Antonio but also got the small-town life that he loved. He missed that when he lived in Huntsville, Alabama, and following Whiskey's family was a no-brainer for him. He was close to the border for quick trips down to Mexico, but still, far enough from the town he and Whiskey grew up in not to be bothered by the ghosts of his past.

Whiskey had set up this little date, telling his friend that he had picked a woman he knew he'd be interested in. So help him, if Whiskey was busting his balls and setting him up to fall on his face, he'd beat the shit out of the guy. It didn't matter to him that Whiskey was almost double his size, he'd still find a way to beat his ass. Anders settled at the bar on a stool in the back corner so he could keep his back to the wall and his eyes on the door. If a single woman walked in there and seemed to be looking for someone, he could give her the once over before he decided if he wanted to stick it out or hightail it out the side door. He knew that made him sound like an ass, but he didn't care. He was already anxious enough about agreeing to this disastrous idea.

He watched as a sexy little brunette walked into the place and looked around, even smiling over at him. But Anders was quickly disappointed when a big guy in a cowboy hat, trying way too hard to fit in, walked in behind her and wrapped his arm around her waist. Yeah—that one stung a little. He checked his watch for the millionth time and swallowed down the last of his beer. It was his second since he got there, and he was done drinking alone and done waiting on a woman who didn't want to meet him.

"Thanks," Anders said, throwing down two twenties and nodding to the bartender. "Keep the change." He stood to leave and was almost out of the bar when a spunky little redhead came barreling through the double doors, running right into him. Anders wrapped his arms around her body, trying to steady her and when she looked up at him with her big green eyes and her cute little button nose speckled with freckles, he knew exactly who he cradled up against his chest.

"Texas Holloway," he whispered. She leaned into his body and damn if she didn't feel right plastered up against him.

"Hi Anders," she said back. "Long time no see," she teased.

He'd seen her plenty in the last twelve years since they graduated high school, but that involved his nightly dreams and her being naked underneath his body, shouting out his name.

"Yeah," he choked, not knowing what else to say to the sexy fireball. He had a crush on her for all four years of high school and when he finally got the nerve up to ask her to prom, she told him that Whiskey had beat him to it and she was going with him. Yeah, that felt like a fucking punch to the gut, but he bowed out gracefully and even helped his best friend find a cheap tux to rent. Anders sat at home that night sulking—even vowing that when he got to Georgetown, he'd never speak to any of them again, including Whiskey. That was a joke because he broke down and called Whiskey the very next morning, waking him to see how his date went with Texas. When his best friend gave a nonchalant answer, acting as if he didn't give a shit about Anders's walking wet dream, he got pissed off again and told Whiskey to go fuck himself. He didn't talk to his friend for over two weeks, not that Whiskey didn't try to figure out what the hell he did wrong. He didn't do anything wrong—Anders was mad at himself for blowing his chance with Texas. He was a chicken shit who never had the balls to ask her out and when he finally did, it was too late. The question now was did fate drop her back into his life or did he have his best friend to thank for seeing her again? Either way, he wasn't going to fuck things up again and wait too long to ask her out. He learned his lesson the hard way as a teenage kid.

"Go out with me," he whispered.

TEXAS

Texas couldn't believe her bad luck when one of her old high school friends, Whiskey O'Brian, ran into her out of the blue, at the grocery store. He and his beautiful wife and precious baby boy were enough to make her want to gag. Sure, she liked the guy back in the day. She even went to prom with him but that was because he was the only boy to ask her. She had a thing for his best friend, Anders Taylor, but he never asked her. For all she knew she was pining away for a boy who didn't even know that she existed. So, she settled for the next best thing and went to prom with his best friend and then talked incessantly about Anders. When the dance was over, most of the kids went to after-parties, but Whiskey insisted on taking her home and who could blame the guy? What guy in his right mind would want to hang out with a girl who talked about his best friend like he was the best thing since sliced bread? The last person on the planet she wanted to run into was Whiskey

O'Brian, but when it came to the universe listening to what she wanted, she had given up.

He told her all about how he and his sexy-as-sin new wife and son just moved to the area, and then he dropped the bomb that Anders had moved back not too long ago himself. She tried to play it cool, but she was sure she was coming off as corny as that teenage girl who followed him around the halls of the high school day in and day out. She told Whiskey that she had been living in the area for almost five years now and no—she wasn't married or even with someone for that matter. Texas didn't miss the looks of pity exchanged by Whiskey and his new missus. Yeah—she got it, she was a total loser and would never be as happy as they seemed to be. Whatever.

She made some lame excuse about having to be on her way because she was just there to pick up a loaf of bread for her peanut butter and jelly sandwich—which was going to be her dinner for the third night in a row, but she wasn't about to tell Whiskey and his beautiful blushing bride that fact. No, she needed to keep things calm, cool, and collected because that's the way she liked to play things. It was who she was—well, who she wanted to be but that was beside the point. She waved at them as she made her way to the register. She felt good about the way she had "adulted" after seeing the guy who took her to prom and couldn't seem to get away from her fast enough. She handled herself like a pro, given the circumstances.

But, then she made the mistake of glancing over to where Whiskey and his wifey were having a heated whispering match and sighed, knowing that he was spilling all the gory details about her one night of complete humiliation and judging from the sympathetic looks coming from his new judgey soul mate—

she was going to have to face them both down and have another (adult) conversation.

"Um," the bombshell brunette murmured. God, what was her name again—oh yeah, Luciana.

"Hi Luciana," Texas breathed, pretty damn proud of herself for remembering the woman's name.

"Hi," she said back. "Listen, I know it's not my place but I'm going to stick my butt in here." Whiskey barked out his laugh and pulled his wife into his side.

"It's not your butt you're sticking into her business, Honey. It's your nose. You are sticking your nose where it does not belong," he said.

"Yes," Luciana said. "Thank you for that correction, Darling." Texas had never been married but she was pretty sure that Luciana's use of the word "Darling" wasn't meant as an endearment. Texas giggled and Whiskey shrugged.

"As I was saying," she continued. "I'd like to stick my nose in your business. You see, Whiskey said that you had a crush on Anders in high school." Texas shot Whiskey a look to let him know she wanted to stab him repeatedly and he had the nerve to shrug again.

"I didn't think it was a secret, Texas. You did talk about him throughout our entire date," Whiskey defended.

"Okay, fine. I admit I used to have a thing for Anders Taylor but that was a long time ago. He's probably moved on and forgotten that I even existed." Yeah, she sounded like a pouty baby, but she couldn't help it. It still kind of stung that she carried around her unrequited love for four whole years.

"Well, he hasn't," Luciana said, interrupting her internal monologue. "Moved on, that is. He's here in this new town and all alone. Whiskey and I have each other and well, it would be nice for Anders to get out and go on a date. So, how about it?" Luciana asked.

"How about what?" Texas questioned.

"Let us set you up on a date with Anders," Whiskey said, trying to help speed things along. He was holding his son and the baby started to fuss.

"Like a blind date?" Texas asked, trying not to sound too enthusiastic or hopeful. But, God, she wanted to go on this date with Anders. She wanted her chance to finally tell him that she wasn't that same geek in high school who used to follow him around, pining for him. She hated that she never got her chance to tell him yes—to go on a real date with him. Hell, she wanted just one good-night kiss from Anders Taylor and now just might be her chance.

"Wait," she said. "Is he still cute?" Not that it mattered but the boy she remembered had to have grown up into one fine-ass man. There would be no way that Anders grew up to be ugly. Whiskey pulled out his cell phone and handed his son over to Luciana. He thumbed through some pictures and found one of just him and Anders, holding the phone out for Texas to see.

"Wow," she mouthed, studying the picture of the two handsome guys. Anders was even better than she had imagined in her nightly fantasies. His dark hair and blue eyes had always drawn her in but she had to admit that she liked the beard—it was a nice addition.

"So—how about it?" Whiskey asked.

She shrugged, trying for casual once again even though she felt like she could burst into flames. "All right," she said. Texas took Whiskey's phone from his hands and typed in her name and phone number. "I'm free this Thursday. Just text me the details." She got back in line at the register and paid for her items, waving to Whiskey and his family on her way out. She didn't want to give him the chance to change his mind, and she high-tailed it out of that grocery store as fast as her legs could carry her.

Now, she was pressed up against Ander's chest, waiting for him to make the next move. At least he seemed to remember her but everything else felt like a blur since she ran into him.

"Go out with me?" he asked and all she could seem to do was nod her head.

"Um wait—isn't that why we are here?" she asked when her brain finally caught up on the events of the last two minutes. He didn't make a move to release her and she was just fine with that. Being plastered up against him wasn't a hardship. She liked the way she could feel every hard inch of Anders. He certainly grew up in all the right places, that was for sure.

"You're my blind date?" Anders asked. "Fucking Whiskey," he grumbled.

"If this wasn't what you expected—if you wanted someone else to show up here tonight, just say the word, Anders." She tried to pull free from him, but he only tightened his arms around her body.

"No—that's not what I meant, Texas. Whiskey didn't give me any clue who I was meeting tonight. I'm just surprised is all," he admitted.

"Good surprise—like you're parents left for the weekend and gave you permission to use the car and have a big party or bad surprise—like you walked in to find your grandparents having sex?" she asked.

Anders chuckled, "Definitely the part where I get the keys to the car and get to have an epic party. Although neither has ever happened to me."

"Well, consider yourself lucky—I had both happen and the clean-up after the party was no fun," she teased.

"Wait—did you walk in on your grandparents having sex?" he asked.

"Yes, and it wasn't for the faint of heart—I'll leave it at that," she said, grimacing.

"It's really good to see you again," Anders whispered.

"You too," she agreed. "So, about this blind date—are we going to go for it or cross paths like two ships in the night?" She was hoping that he'd agree to continue with their date, but she suddenly felt so unsure of herself.

"I'm not sure where you come up with these things," he said. "But I'd like to try the whole blind date thing if you're game." Anders watched her as if waiting for an answer and Texas realized he was still holding her against his body.

"Only if you promise to kiss me goodnight at the end of the date," she whispered.

"Oh, Honey—I'll kiss you good morning too, if you'll let me," Anders' growled. Yeah—it was some good luck that she ran into her old high school friend, Whiskey, at the grocery store.

Texas sat across from Anders, wondering how she ended up having dinner with her high school crush, and the steak that she ordered suddenly seemed unappetizing. She wanted to play it cool and at least pretend not to be freaking out over the fact that she was on a blind date with a man she'd been fantasizing about since high school. But cool was eluding her and instead, she sat across from Anders struck mute and feeling foolish for agreeing to go on this date in the first place.

"You're awfully quiet," Anders said. "I don't remember you being this quiet when we were younger." Her nervous laugh filled the corner of the bar that they were sitting in and she shook her head like a loon.

"I guess I'm just a little nervous," she admitted. Honesty was her only excuse because coming up with a lie on the fly wasn't an option for her right now. Texas was usually good in stressful situations but for some reason, sitting across from the hottest guy in her high school class was rendering her speechless.

Anders reached across the table and took her hand into his own and her stomach did a little flip flop. "It's just me, Texas," he breathed.

"That might be the problem," she mumbled.

"Problem?" Anders asked.

"Well, you probably know that I had a crush on you back in high school. I mean—I'm guessing that Whiskey told you how I went on and on about you when he took me to prom, like a complete idiot," she said.

"Um, no," Anders breathed. "He never mentioned anything about that night. Honestly, I always wondered what happened that he didn't ask you out again."

"That was my fault," she griped. "I might have rambled on about you like a lunatic. God, I had such a crush on you," she gushed.

"I never knew," Anders said. "When I finally got up the nerve to ask you to prom, you said you were going with Whiskey. I just assumed that you liked him."

"Nope," she admitted. "Not at all. In fact, the only reason I went with him was because he was the only guy who asked me. Well, that and the fact that he was your best friend, and I was hoping that somehow, you'd notice me if you saw me with him. Stupid, I know," she grumbled.

"Actually, it worked," Anders admitted. "I was jealous as fuck."

"Really?" Texas asked. She sat forward as if Anders was going to share a secret and he smiled at her, making her girl parts gooey.

"Yep," he admitted. "I sat at home during prom and sulked the entire night. The next morning, I called Whiskey, and he was so cryptic about your night together that I didn't speak to him for weeks. But he never told me exactly what happened. It was worse not knowing how things went than to have Whiskey's cryptic explanation of your date. My mind of course wandered to the worst-case scenario."

"Which was?" she asked.

"Which was that he had sex with you and was dumping you. I wanted to beat the shit out of him. Hell, I went to college madder than hell that he took you out, but I eventually forgave him. You became the one who got away," he almost whispered.

"Why didn't you ever look me up?" she asked.

"Because of my job, really. I joined the FBI and well, I'm not in one place for very long. Plus, my job is dangerous, and I never thought that would warrant me a relationship, so I never tried to have one," he admitted.

"Do you still travel a lot?" she asked.

"Yes," Anders said. "Whiskey and I are on the same team and we're leaving in the morning for a case."

"Are you allowed to tell me where you're going or is that classified?" she teased.

"Not really," he said. "I mean, I can tell you that I'm going to Mexico, but I might have to kill you." Texas couldn't help her girly laughter that filled the air around them. God, she was being such a cliché tonight. Pulling off nervous schoolgirl wasn't usually in her wheelhouse, but tonight, she played the role perfectly.

"How long will you be gone?" she asked. "On your trip to Mexico."

Anders shrugged, "Not sure," he breathed. "Could be a few days to a week, maybe more. Why?" he asked.

Now it was her turn to shrug her answer. "Just wondering if or when I'll get my second date." She watched him, waiting for him to protest giving her another date and when he smiled at her, Anders nearly took her breath away. It was something he'd always been able to do. He had this way about him—something that made her think of a cowboy mixed with a little bit of bad boy biker. Whatever it was, he completely turned her on, and not getting another chance with him wasn't something she wanted to think about.

"How about next Saturday?" Anders asked.

"But I thought you didn't know when you'd be back in town," Texas protested. He was giving her exactly what she wanted, and she was trying to talk him out of it.

"I'll have a jet at my disposal and can catch a flight home for the weekend, as long as I have a reason to come home," he said. "Want to be my reason to come home, Texas?" Anders asked.

She didn't even have to consider her answer—she knew it before the words were even out of her mouth. "Yes," she breathed. "I'd love to go out with you again next Saturday, Anders," Texas agreed.

"Then it's settled," he said. Anders checked his watch and frowned. "I hate to cut the night short, but I do have an early morning flight."

"Oh," she breathed, suddenly feeling very self-conscious again. Texas wondered just what Anders was going to want from her at the end of their date. He had hinted at kissing her in the morning, but they were nowhere near ready to spend the night together. She only just found him again and she didn't want to rush things with Anders.

"I'm sorry," he apologized.

"No," she said. "I don't mind. I have an early morning too," she said.

"Please tell me that you're an undercover spy and you have a secret mission to go on," Anders teased. Texas was sure he was going to find her a whole lot more boring than that once she told him what she did for a living.

"I'm definitely not a spy," she giggled. "I'm a preschool teacher," she said. "I work with four-year-olds."

"Wow," Anders breathed. "I never pegged you as someone who would want to work with kids," he said.

"Really?" she asked. "What did you imagine I'd turn out to be?" Anders smiled at her again and stroked his thumb over her hand and she thought that was the sweetest gesture.

"Well, I thought you'd be a scientist or something like that. I remember sitting next to you in biology and I remember you loving that class," he said.

Texas giggled, "Yeah well if we're being completely honest here, that had more to do with who I was sitting next to and less to do with the subject being taught. Heck, I studied my ass off for that class."

"Oh," Anders said. "I see. Well, if we're going with complete honesty, I copied off you quite a few times, so I appreciate you studying that sweet little ass off for biology, Honey."

"I knew it," she said. "I knew you were copying off of me, I just didn't care," she said.

"I appreciate that," Anders said. "If it wasn't for you, I wouldn't have passed that class and gotten into college."

"Glad I could help," Texas laughed.

Anders paid their bill and walked her out to her car, her stomach roiling with nervous butterflies. "So, next Saturday?" she asked.

"Yep," Anders said, sounding just as nervous as she felt. "Can I pick you up or do you want to meet me again?" he asked.

"Um, I guess I can trust that you're not a serial killer," she teased. "I don't usually give guys my address or let them pick me up for a date, but you seem to be a pretty standup guy. Here, give me your phone," she ordered. Anders trustingly handed it over and she put in her cell number. "There, now you have my number. Just text me the details and I'll be ready."

"Looks can be deceiving, Honey," he breathed.

"Sorry?" She asked, trying to keep up with him.

"You said that I seem like a standup guy. Looks can be deceiving," he explained. He was standing so close to her; she could feel his breath on her face.

"Good to know," she whispered. "You gonna kiss me, Anders?" she asked.

"Yes," he breathed. He was so much taller than she was, he pulled her up against his body and lifted her off the ground. He kissed her, sealing his mouth over hers and when she moaned into his mouth, he licked his way in, letting his tongue find hers. It was the hottest kiss she'd ever received and the fact that it was from Anders was everything. When he stopped kissing her, she was breathless, panting, and ready for more.

"Good night, Texas," Anders whispered. He opened her car

door and waited for her to get in. She wasn't sure if she wanted to protest or slip into the driver's seat and speed away as quickly as possible. Nothing was going as she had envisioned and now, he was all but dismissing her.

Texas slipped into her car and Anders shut her door. Before she drove off, she chanced one last look in her rearview mirror, and he waved at her. Yeah, her first date with Anders was nothing like she expected it would be. All she would be able to do was overanalyze everything that happened during their dinner and then obsessively plan everything she hoped to say and do on Saturday's date because she wanted their second date to be perfect.

ANDERS

Anders was packed, dressed, and ready to hit the road by six in the morning. He knew that Whiskey would be ready, but he still needed to talk to him. Anders called Whiskey and when he answered his cell, he didn't know if he should cuss him out or thank him for setting him up with Texas. He wanted her during high school, and he knew Whisky would remember that but having her meet him at the bar was above and beyond being his best friend.

"What the fuck, man?" Anders asked.

"I take it she showed up then?" Whiskey asked. "I can't take all the credit for the blind date idea," Whiskey said. "It was mostly Luciana's handy work. My wife can be pretty crafty when she wants to be."

"Yeah—as in witchcraft. And yes, Texas showed up for our date. A head's up would have been great, man," Anders said.

"Now, where would the fun in that be? I mean, you work best under pressure and I knew that if I had told you that Texas was your blind date, you wouldn't have shown up," Whiskey explained.

"Yes, I would have," Anders defended. He was totally lying and if he knew his best friend, Whiskey would know it too. He never got away with anything concerning Whiskey. They called each other on their bullshit and Anders wouldn't have it any other way.

"You're a fucking awful liar," Whiskey grumbled. "Why are you calling me so early?" he asked. "We still have two hours before I meet you at the hangar." Whisky had his own plane, and he was one of the only pilots Anders trusted when he headed out on a mission—especially one as covert as the one they were going. He was still hoping that his meeting with his guy on the inside of the Camillo family went according to plan. The last time they made the trip down, Angel didn't show up and they had to return to Texas with nothing.

"I'm just anxious to get on the road," he admitted. "I have a bad feeling about this trip and the sooner we can get down there and meet with Angel, the sooner I can get home."

"To see Texas again?" Whiskey prodded. He knew that he'd end up giving Whiskey the full details about their date at some point, but he was an ass and loved to see his friend squirm a little. He'd let Whiskey stew and maybe even beg a little before he gave him the details.

"None of your business, man," Anders said. Whiskey couldn't see his smile through the phone, but he was pretty sure his friend would be able to hear it.

"All right, I don't have time for your games right now. Pick me up in an hour and we can head out a little early." Whiskey didn't wait for him to agree to his orders, he just ended the call and Anders chuckled.

He checked his emails and just as he was about to pocket his cell, a message came through from Texas.

Had a great time last night at dinner. Can't wait to see you on Saturday—safe trip.

Anders smiled at her message and decided to shoot her back a quick response before he overthought whether or not that was being too aggressive and seeming too eager. He wanted to play things cool with her but that wasn't his style. Honestly, he was completely unsure what to do about sexy Texas literally falling into his life last night. The only thing he was sure of was that he couldn't wait to get this trip over with so he could see her again.

I had a good time too. I'll text you when I get back this week and we can plan a time for Saturday—looking forward to it.

Anders thought about putting a bunch of exclamation marks at the end of his sentence but decided against it since that would probably have him coming off sounding like a complete goober. Yeah, he was excited about seeing Texas again, and getting through the next few days was going to be hell. At least she gave him something to look forward to and this time, when she kissed him goodnight, he wouldn't let her get into her car and drive away from him. This time, he'd drag her off to his bed and finally get what he wanted—his chance with Texas Holloway.

The Lonestar Rangers Six Book Box set Universal Link->

ABOUT K.L. RAMSEY & BE KELLY

Romance Rebel fighting for
Happily Ever After!

K. L. Ramsey currently resides in West Virginia (Go Mountaineers!). In her spare time, she likes to read romance novels, go to WVU football games and attend book club (aka-drink wine) with girlfriends. K. L. enjoys writing Contemporary Romance, Erotic Romance, and Sexy Ménage! She loves to write strong, capable women and bossy, hot as hell alphas, who fall ass over tea kettle for them. And of course, her stories always have a happy ending. But wait—there's more!

Somewhere along the writing path, K.L. developed a love of ALL things paranormal (but has a special affinity for shifters <YUM!!>)!! She decided to take a chance and create another persona- BE Kelly- to bring you all of her yummy shifters, seers, and everything paranormal (plus a hefty dash of MC!).

K. L. RAMSEY'S SOCIAL MEDIA

Ramsey's Rebels - K.L. Ramsey's Readers Group
https://www.facebook.com/groups/ramseysrebels

KL Ramsey & BE Kelly's ARC Team
https://www.facebook.com/groups/klramseyandbekellyarcteam

KL Ramsey and BE Kelly's Newsletter
https://mailchi.mp/4e73ed1b04b9/authorklramsey/

KL Ramsey and BE Kelly's Website
https://www.klramsey.com

- facebook.com/kl.ramsey.58
- instagram.com/itsprivate2
- bookbub.com/profile/k-l-ramsey
- twitter.com/KLRamsey5
- amazon.com/K.L.-Ramsey/e/B0799P6JGJ

BE KELLY'S SOCIAL MEDIA

BE Kelly's Reader's group
https://www.facebook.com/groups/kellsangelsreadersgroup/

- facebook.com/be.kelly.564
- instagram.com/bekellyparanormalromanceauthor
- twitter.com/BEKelly9
- bookbub.com/profile/be-kelly
- amazon.com/BE-Kelly/e/B081LLD38M

WORKS BY K. L. RAMSEY

The Relinquished Series Box Set

Love Times Infinity

Love's Patient Journey

Love's Design

Love's Promise

Harvest Ridge Series Box Set

Worth the Wait

The Christmas Wedding

Line of Fire

Torn Devotion

Fighting for Justice

Last First Kiss Series Box Set

Theirs to Keep

Theirs to Love

Theirs to Have

Theirs to Take

Second Chance Summer Series

True North

The Wrong Mister Right

Ties That Bind Series

Saving Valentine

Blurred Lines

Dirty Little Secrets

Ties That Bind Box Set

Taken Series

Double Bossed

Double Crossed

Double The Mistletoe

Double Down

Owned

His Secret Submissive

His Reluctant Submissive

His Cougar Submissive

His Nerdy Submissive

His Stubborn Submissive

Owned Series Boxset

Alphas in Uniform

Hellfire

Finding His Destiny

Guilty Until Proven Innocent

Royal Bastards MC

Savage Heat

Whiskey Tango

Can't Fix Cupid

Ratchet's Revenge

Patched for Christmas

Love at First Fight

Dizzy's Desire

Possessing Demon

Mistletoe and Mayhem

Bullseye- Struck by Cupid's Arrow

Legend

Spider

Blade's Christmas Ride

Savage Hell MC Series

Roadkill

REPOssession

Dirty Ryder

Hart's Desire

Axel's Grind

Razor's Edge

Trista's Truth

Thorne's Rose

Lone Star Rangers

Don't Mess With Texas

Sweet Adeline

Dash of Regret

Austin's Starlet

Ranger's Revenge

Heart of Stone

Smokey Bandits MC Series

Aces Wild

Queen of Hearts

Full House

King of Clubs

Joker's Wild

Betting on Blaze

Tirana Brothers (Social Rejects Syndicate

Llir

Altin

Veton

Tirana Brothers Boxset

Dirty Desire Series

Torrid

Clean Sweep

No Limits

Mountain Men Mercenary Series

Eagle Eye

Hacker

Widowmaker

Deadly Sins Syndicate (Mafia Series)

Pride

Envy

Greed

Lust

Wrath

Sloth

Gluttony

Deadly Sins Syndicate Boxset

Forgiven Series

Confession of a Sinner

Confessions of a Saint

Confessions of a Rebel

Chasing Serendipity Series

Kismet

Sealed With a Kiss Series

Kissable

Never Been Kissed

Garo Syndicate Trilogy

Edon

Bekim

Rovena

Garo Syndicate Boxset

Billionaire Boys Club

His Naughty Assistant

His Virgin Assistant

His Nerdy Assistant

His Curvy Assistant

His Bossy Assistant

His Rebellious Assistant

Billionaire Boys Club Six Book Boxset

Grumpy Mountain Men Series

Grizz

Jed

Axel

A Grumpy Mountain Man for Xmas

The Bridezilla Series

Happily Ever After- Almost

Picture Perfect

Haunted Honeymoon for One

Rope 'Em and Ride 'Em Series

Saddle Up

A Cowboy for Christmas

Summer Lovin' Series

Beach Rules

Making Waves

Endless Summer

The Bound Series

Bound by Her Mafia Bosses

Bound by His Mafia Princess

Dirty Riders MC Series

Riding Hard

Riding Dirty

Riding Steel

The Dirty Daddies Series

Doctor Daddy

Baby Daddy

A Princess for Daddy

A Daddy for Christmas

The Kink Club Series

Salacious

Insatiable

WORKS BY BE KELLY (K.L.'S ALTER EGO...)

Reckoning MC Seer Series
Reaper

Tank

Raven

Reckoning MC Series Box Set

Perdition MC Shifter Series
Ringer

Rios

Trace

Perdition 3 Book Box Set

Silver Wolf Shifter Series
Daddy Wolf's Little Seer

Daddy Wolf's Little Captive

Daddy Wolf's Little Star

Rogue Enforcers
Juno

Blaze

Elite Enforcers
A Very Rogue Christmas Novella

One Rogue Turn

Graystone Academy Series

Eden's Playground

Violet's Surrender

Holly's Hope (A Christmas Novella)

Renegades Shifter Series

Pandora's Promise

Kinsley's Pact

Leader of the Pack Series

Wren's Pack

Made in United States
North Haven, CT
11 March 2025